CASS TELL

THE LAST JERUSALEM

An End Times Odyssey in a World Aflame

destinēe

Books by Cass Tell

Novels and Novellas
The Last Jerusalem
Faraway Lands
The Hot Pepper Mystery – a Sarah Zipper novella
Naked Island
The Coffee Lover – a Sarah Zipper novel
Dance With Poetic Sea
The Savant
The Cookbook
Pale Tides
A Smile Forever, A novella, and short stories
Virtual Eyes
Social Code
Blue Fate 5: Pursuit
Blue Fate 4: Squeeze
Blue Fate 3: Dropout
Blue Fate 2: Buyout
Blue Fate 1: Startup

Wings Series - Novellas
The Brussels Atonement – Wings Series 5
The London Inferno – Wings Series 4
The Paris Crossing – Wings Series 3
The Prague Transit – Wings Series 2
The Munich Shift – Wings Series 1, The Beginning

Children's and Teens Stories
Street Smart: Run Fast, Rise Strong
The Insidious Hope - Amy and Jack – Series 4
The Impossible Storm - Amy and Jack – Series 3
The Amazing Rescuers - Amy and Jack – Series 2
The Impossible Prize - Amy and Jack – Series 1
The Wise Girl and Baba Yaga's Son

Copyright

THE LAST JERUSALEM: An End Times Odyssey in a World Aflame
By CASS TELL

Published by Destinée Media www.destineemedia.com
Written by Cass Tell www.casstell.com
Cover concept by Per-Ole Lind www.perolelind.com
Cover image by the author using Bing AI

ISBN: 978-1-938367-91-5

Contents

Chapter 1

The morning began as usual, leaving home before dawn, a brief bus ride through the winding roads of Jerusalem, and the familiar walk through the narrow, cobblestone streets of the Old City. But today, the air felt different.

The rising sun cast a soft, golden glow over the Temple Mount, illuminating the ancient stones that had witnessed generations of prayers, miracles, and wars. As I made my way to the hut near the excavation site for my first cup of coffee, the unexpected happened.

A distant boom reverberated through the city, shaking the ground beneath my feet, and it took me a moment to orient myself.

Because of the worrying events taking place around this country, it was more than a blast. It felt as though history itself had sent a shockwave through time, stirring echoes of a prophecy I had never thought I would witness. Something ancient and foreboding had been set in motion, a truth so powerful it could no longer be ignored. I knew what this could mean. I had studied the texts and the signs, but the rational side of me still doubted. Could this indeed be the prophesied end? The great war foretold in scripture? The final clash that would engulf the world?

Standing there, stunned by the suddenness of it all, the reality strikes me with chilling clarity. Nations are aligning, surrounding this small country like wolves circling their prey, each vying for a piece of land bathed in millennia of bloodshed. As an archaeologist, I have always been focused on the past, piecing together fragments of history. I never imagined I would find myself in the middle of the very prophecies I had only read about.

In my backpack, I carry a small, worn edition of the Holy Bible. It speaks of times like these—when kings rise and fall, armies gather, and the fate of the world is decided on this very ground. Now, it seems, the words are becoming reality. The King of the North, a ruthless and power-hungry tyrant, is on the move, marching toward Jerusalem with an army of hostile nations at his back. A storm is brewing—one that will reshape the world, leaving nothing but ruins in its wake.

One verse, in particular, echoes in my mind: *"Demonic spirits go out to the kings of the world, to gather them for the battle on the great day of God Almighty."* Other verses point to the same cataclysmic event. Could this really be happening?

Israel's army is strong, yet even it faces impossible odds against the overwhelming forces closing in. It feels as though the David and Goliath story is being rewritten—but this time, the stakes are far greater.

I, Thomas Thornton, a thirty-seven-year-old archaeologist with a passion for ancient history, am now swept up in the turmoil of this unfolding chaos. For years, I have worked alongside Israeli scholars, excavating near the Temple Mount, unearthing artifacts that connect the Jewish people to this sacred land. But now, the past seems irrelevant compared to the terrifying present. The peace Israel had managed to secure with its neighbors has unraveled in a matter of months, replaced by hatred and tension. Something far beyond politics seems to be at play—an almost supernatural force compelling nations to act.

As diplomats scramble to maintain peace, the world holds its breath. For a while, it seems like the storm will pass. Then, only days ago, a single gunshot shattered the fragile calm. In an instant, armies mobilize, and the specter of war looms once more.

Our archaeological team has been so engrossed in our work that we are oblivious to the rising conflict beyond the city walls. We are scholars focused on history, not geopolitics. But perhaps we have been blind fools who fail to recognize the signs.

As I hurriedly finish my coffee, Tal, one of my colleagues, arrives with a grim expression. He is followed by our leader, Dr.

Schlomo Peretz. "Did you hear that boom?" Peretz asks, his voice tight and concerned.

"Yes," Tal and I reply in unison.

Tal, who is responsible for cataloging artifacts, adds, "There were military movements last night. The northern army is advancing through Syria."

My heart sinks. The peace agreement, which had required all armies to withdraw, has clearly been violated. And now, war seems inevitable.

Dr. Peretz's face darkens. "We should abandon the dig for today. Tal, you need to get to your family. Make sure they're safe and check in with your military unit."

Tal nods, his eyes filled with worry. He is married with two young children, and like most Israeli men, he serves in the military reserves. He leaves quickly, and before Dr. Peretz can follow, I ask, "What about you?"

"I'll move my family to our home in the Judean hills. It has a basement I've turned into a bunker. After that, I'll see how I can help." He pauses, his voice trembling. "If this is the great battle before the Day of the Lord, then Jerusalem will be attacked. History shows us what happens when this city is besieged."

I watch him hurry away, feeling more lost than ever. I have no family here and no military or civil responsibilities. I have never believed these ancient prophecies would happen in my lifetime. Peretz, on the other hand, has always taken them literally. Perhaps I am the one who has been the fool.

As I wander south through the narrow streets of the Old City, my thoughts race. Armies are advancing, nations are gathering, and the puzzle pieces are falling into place. Fear creeps in, but alongside it comes a strange sense of purpose. The texts I have studied for so long seem to take on new meaning. Are we really living in the end-times? Is this the Apocalypse? I need answers.

The streets are unrecognizable, with shops closed and merchants gone. The panicked masses flee through the narrow ancient alleyways. A second boom echoes in the distance, followed by screams. Is it a missile? A bomb? It doesn't matter. Chaos reigns.

Ahead, a Hasidic Jew stumbles and falls, trampled by the frantic masses. Urgency grips me, and I fight through the crowd to help him. His eyes, full of years and wisdom, meet mine with silent gratitude as I lift him to his feet. He whispers, *"Toda raba,"* thank you, his voice barely audible amidst the chaos.

But there is something more in his gaze—an unease, a hesitation. To him, my touch might be an impurity, something that violates his deeply held beliefs. Yet, in that moment, I feel a connection. We are both caught in the same storm, both trying to make sense of a world unraveling around us.

He disappears into the crowd, and I press on, my mind racing. Is this indeed the beginning of the end? Have I missed the signs all along? For years, I have studied the Bible as history, not prophecy. Now, I wish I had paid more attention to the future it foretold. Although Hasidic has spent his life studying the holy text, I wonder if he feels the same.

As I navigate the maze of streets, the ground trembles beneath my feet. This time, it was an earthquake. Jerusalem has always been susceptible to quakes, but this feels different. The shaking intensifies the crowd's panic, and I realize how fragile everything truly is.

Ahead, a stone building has collapsed into a pile of rubble. Is it from the quake or an attack? The question barely matters.

With each step, the words of Jesus echo in my mind: *"When you see Jerusalem surrounded by armies, you will know its desolation is near. Then let those in Judea flee to the mountains."* Is this my sign to leave? Should I run for the hills, like Dr. Peretz?

I have a rugged SUV parked at my home on the southern edge of the city, a vehicle used for desert expeditions. Now, it might be my only ticket to safety. But the question remains: should I flee or wait and see what unfolds?

For now, all I can do is keep moving forward—toward home, toward the unknown.

Chapter 2

The usual hum of the Old City, with its ceaseless flow of life, is different today, as if someone has jammed a stick into an anthill. The frenzy is intense.

The streets in the Old City are narrow, but now they feel particularly suffocating. Moving through the crowd, I can't escape the nagging sense of fragility, the fleeting nature of this existence. Behind the hectic scene, a storm of a far greater magnitude has been brewing for months. War looms as armies gather around Israel like predators around wounded prey, each driven by greed and the hunger for dominance.

Few believe it would come to this. We assume the politicians, in their self-proclaimed wisdom, will pull us back from the brink. But their failure is evident in the panicked faces around me. It feels like a greater force is at play, something in the ethereal world pulling nations to a horrible encounter.

Exiting the Old City of Jerusalem, I see that the route to my house is clogged, buses motionless in traffic, as if paralyzed by impending doom. I have no choice but to walk. Changing course, I thread my way south, skirting the Temple Mount, heading toward the east side of the city where the Kidron Valley stretches out like a vast, ancient artery.

I quicken my pace, feeling the sweat mix with the dust of the city. The streets here are no better—cars abandoned, some people wandering, their eyes lifted to the sky, searching for answers or hope. Above us, fighter jets rip through the heavens, their engines roaring like angry gods. I can't tell if they belong to the Israeli Air Force or to some hostile nation closing in. It's impossible to know anymore.

When I finally reach the Kidron Valley, a strange sense of reverence creeps over me. This ground has seen it all—kings, prophets, and battles of ancient times. King David fled through this valley during Absalom's revolt, and King Hezekiah defended Jerusalem from here. It's as though the earth itself carries their memories. Joel's prophecy flashes in my mind—this is the place where nations will gather for the final reckoning. And if I remember correctly, in the Book of Revelation, John envisions a river of blood flowing from this very valley. Could that be more than a symbol? The thought unsettles me.

With one last look back at the Old City, I force myself to march southward toward my home.

Suddenly, the sky explodes with the deafening roar of jet engines, tearing through the thick air like thunderclaps of war. I freeze, my heart slamming against my ribs. High above me, two jets dance in a deadly ballet, one launching a missile with a streak of vapor in its wake. The other swerves hard, trying desperately to dodge the attack. Then comes the flash—a blinding, brilliant light—followed by a muffled boom. One of the jets begins its doomed spiral toward the earth, trailing thick black smoke as it disappears to the east beyond the Mount of Olives, a wounded beast falling from the sky.

For a moment, time seems to stand still. Then, from the cloud of destruction, a small parachute blooms in the sky. The pilot ejected, floating downward like a single feather against the blue expanse. The vast theater of war has reduced itself to one man's fragile descent—an image that will haunt me, the human cost of conflict laid bare.

I stand rooted to the spot, staring up at that lone pilot, my mind racing. Surely, someone—somewhere—has the sense to stop this madness before it consumes us all. Why is this small, rocky patch of land so important? What could justify the catastrophic price of war? There are resources here, of course— oil and gas under the sea—but it seems far too small a reason to provoke this much destruction. Unless there is something deeper pulling the strings. My years of studying ancient history have taught me that the motivations behind great conflicts often aren't rational. They are spiritual. And nothing in this world has the power to twist logic like a force we can't see.

I swallow hard, a knot tightening in my chest. The horror unfolding around me is more real than any artifact I have ever uncovered. This is no excavation, no historical curiosity—it is happening, and I am standing in the middle of it.

My thoughts turn to my house, just a few miles away, nestled on the outskirts of the city. I need to get there, to think, to plan. The heaviness of history, prophecy, and fear presses down on me, urging me to move faster. I pick up my pace, determined to reach whatever safety my home might offer before the storm fully breaks.

Chapter 3

News passes from mouth to ear in short, urgent exchanges on the street. Weeks ago, people would barely make eye contact. Now, absolute strangers exchange information as though hoping for the slightest signal of good news. But discerning truth from imagination is a futile endeavor.

I hear someone mention the enormous armies of the world mobilizing in Lebanon and Syria. Another colossal army gathers in Iraq, and yet another is in the south beyond Suez. Could this indeed be the Day of the Lord inching toward its prophesied end? It feels as though all the world's forces are converging on this ancient land for a final reckoning.

Through the noise and confusion, I see soldiers moving purposefully, their steps firm and faces grim. Men and women alike, their uniforms blending into the city's worn-out streets, carry weapons with a resolve that chills my blood. These aren't the faces of fear; they're the faces of people who have lived with war for generations. This is their response, their defiance, the embodiment of "Never Again." They aren't just defending their homes; they're standing against annihilation. Yet I can't shake the sickening realization that many of these determined faces will soon vanish, consumed by the coming storm.

The spiritual implications gnaw at me. How could any divine force allow such destruction? My grandfather often spoke of a new heaven and a new earth, a promised time when all of this would pass. But that promise feels distant and abstract now as I weave through panicked crowds under the brutal sun. In the heat and chaos, those words seem as far away as the stars.

I keep moving, sticking to my plan. Four kilometers separate me from my house, a distance that seems to stretch further with each passing moment. But now, I have another destination in mind before home—the U.S. Embassy, which stands between me and my final goal. Maybe there, in the heart of American presence, I can find help or at least information.

As I approach the embassy, the sight of American soldiers stationed at the gate brings a flicker of hope. They stand tall, weapons in hand, their presence a reminder of a distant power in a world unraveling. I step forward, desperation biting at my words.

"I'm American," I tell the nearest soldier. "Are they evacuating U.S. citizens?"

The soldier's face remains impassive. "We don't have any clear information right now," he says. "It's looking bad. A full-blown war could start any minute. This morning, a roadside bomb cut off the road to Ben Gurion Airport. No flights are leaving, and no one's getting there."

"What's your exit plan?" I press, hoping for some direction, any direction.

He shakes his head, his jaw tightening. "It's getting narrower by the minute. We're not sure."

Before I can respond, a deafening screech splits the air. Then comes the blast, a crushing explosion that shakes the ground and sends a ball of fire rolling through one corner of the embassy. The earth quivers beneath me, and instinctively, I grab the fence for support, my heart racing as I scan the destruction. Flames lick the air, the far end of the embassy burning in a violent spectacle.

The soldier turns to me, his expression grim. "That answers your question," he says, his voice stern with finality. "There's no refuge here. You're on your own. Good luck."

Without waiting for more, he and the other soldiers run toward the parking lot, where two of their comrades lie motionless on the ground. I don't hesitate. I bolt, fear driving my legs as I sprint away from the burning embassy, my mind racing faster than my feet. More missiles will come; I can feel it in my bones.

How will the Americans respond to this? While it still has a strong military, for quite some time, the country has been in an economic and moral decline. The current leaders lack courage. So, until now, the United States of America has been on the sidelines. Will the bombing of their embassy provoke action or only empty rhetoric?

Without the support of my country, I must find a way forward. The command of Jesus echoes in my mind. *"Leave Jerusalem."* The words, once an ancient lesson for disciples, now feel like a direct order, urgent and inescapable.

This is no allegory, no abstract scripture. It's reality, and I am no longer a distant observer of prophecy. I'm in it.

The soldier's words haunt me as I run. Even the most robust institutions, even the most fortified embassies, can crumble in an instant. There is no safety. Everything is fragile. I must keep moving and must survive. The idea of hunkering down in my house suddenly feels like a death sentence. I need to leave to get far from the city before the full force of destruction descends.

I race through the streets, the faces of the people around me blurring into a collective mask of fear and determination. The Israelis know war too well. They have been attacked before and have survived, but this feels different. This feels final.

Yet, despite the looming catastrophe, there is a unity in the air, an unspoken resolve that binds them together. I pass a man on his knees, rocking back and forth in fervent prayer, his voice lost in the cacophony of desperation. It's a familiar sight in these parts, a reminder of the power of faith in times of despair. Yet even that seems vulnerable now, as fragile as the world itself.

The sound of gunfire erupts in the distance, sharp and unmistakable. It's impossible to tell who is fighting who anymore.

I run faster, each step carrying me further into the unknown, away from the city that has been my home, into a future I can no longer predict.

Chapter 4

In the tangle of confusion, my survival instincts kick into overdrive. Disorder grips the streets as police wave their arms, shouting in a futile attempt to control the surge of vehicles and panicked citizens. For all the country's notorious lack of discipline, I know they will unite in moments like this. When the outside world threatens, these people band together with an unspoken pact forged in fire and history.

Taking the back streets, I jog through narrow alleys, past ancient stone walls. The journey finally brings me to my doorstep, a modest house nestled near the Archaeological Garden. A place that once represented peace now feels suffocated by the storm raging beyond its walls.

The door creaks as I step inside, and the familiar scents of home greet me like ghosts. There's something off about the air, though. The books lining the shelves, the artifacts carefully displayed—all remnants of a life that now seem as distant as the history they represent. Each piece of furniture, each worn page of a journal, stands frozen in time while the world outside spirals into chaos.

As I stand there, a flood of memories washes over me. My grandfather's legacy seems to hover in the room, as tangible as the relics he's passed down to me. From the age of twelve, I have come to this country every summer to be by his side. We spent long days under the unforgiving sun, uncovering fragments of ancient civilizations. He was my guide, not just in the world of archaeology but in life. His stories were not just about kings and battles; they were about trust, defiance, and consequences.

He died suddenly, leaving me with more than just his stories. An inheritance from him enabled me to buy this house, but it's his wisdom and love for the ancient stones that shaped who I have become. And now, as the world seems to close in, I cling to that memory like a lifeline.

My eyes sweep over the cabinet of archaeological treasures. A pottery handle from Joshua's time. A Philistine bracelet, worn by hands long turned to splintered bone. These are more than objects to me; they are connections to the past, to people who have loved, fought, and survived in this land long before the present conflict. What would they make of the chaos now?

One object, though, holds my gaze longer than the others. A photograph. It's a snapshot of a younger me, standing next to Debbie. A painful reminder of love lost. It's a relic of a different kind—one I have tried to bury deep. Debbie's leaving broke my heart in a way that changed me forever. Other photos of her remain hidden away, but this one sits out in the open, defying my attempts to forget.

Yet it's not Debbie's image I clutch now. Instead, I find myself gripping a smaller frame—a photo of my grandfather and me, both of us smiling, carefree. I slide the picture into my pocket, a token of strength as I prepare for the storm outside.

The garage is my next stop. My SUV waits, ready for action. It has been a dependable companion on countless excavations through harsh desert terrains, and now it will be my refuge. It's fully stocked: gas tanks, water jugs, dried food, and the essentials for survival—a small tent, camping stove, and tiny solar panel—all tucked neatly away. I add the photo of my grandfather to the glove compartment, a final, personal touch amid the cold necessities of survival.

Before leaving, I go through the house, performing simple acts that now feel monumental. I empty the fridge, unplugging it with the irrational hope that one day, I might return to find everything as it was. Then, I remember something crucial—my passport. Digging through my desk, I find it, along with a secret compartment holding a tin box. Inside are Israeli Shekels, US Dollars, gold coins, and jewelry. My mother's engagement ring and diamond wedding ring are in the box, along with the wedding rings of my grandfather and father. My grandfather started this collection, and I have added to it over the years.

I tuck the box into the SUV, lock the garage, and climb into the driver's seat. The engine roars to life, a sound that cuts through the silence of the neighborhood. After leaving the garage, shutting the garage door, and pulling out of the driveway, I can't help but glance back at the house, wondering if I will ever see it again. It feels like I am leaving behind not just bricks and mortar but a part of myself.

The streets ahead are a maze of confusion and blockage. The main road, usually bustling with life, is now sealed off, a blockade of metal and frustration. Turning onto side streets, I wind my way through the southern edges of Jerusalem, where buildings once full of life now stand empty. Shopfronts, abandoned.

Fear gnaws at me, but a strange calm settles in my chest. The verse echoes in my mind. *"When you see Jerusalem surrounded by armies..."* It feels more real than ever before, a prophecy unfolding before my eyes.

As I leave the city, the landscape shifts. Because of the traffic jams on the streets of Jerusalem, I'm forced to go southeast. Open spaces replace the suffocating streets. Ahead lies the road to Bethlehem, a place no less symbolic in this moment of turmoil. The birthplace of the Prince of Peace is now a place of uncertainty. But I know better than to drive directly through it. The chaos there will be no different from the madness I am fleeing. Instead, I veer off onto a dirt road, less traveled, winding its way through the countryside.

As I drive, my thoughts circle back to Bethlehem and the irony of it all. This land, so tied to the hope of peace, is once again a battlefield. The path ahead is uncertain, but then an idea begins to emerge—a place in the desert.

Chapter 5

Leaving Jerusalem, the city shrinks in my rearview mirror, its golden domes and ancient stones growing smaller with every mile. A heavy sadness lodges in my chest—a grief more profound than sorrow. It's as if I'm leaving behind more than stone and mortar. The prophet Zechariah's words echo in my mind, a reminder of Jerusalem's importance in the eyes of the divine: *"For whoever touches you touches the apple of His eye."*

How many times had I walked her streets and felt that inexplicable connection, as though the city breathed with something more than mere history, as if it were alive? Now, with its future ambiguous, I wonder if I'll ever see her again. Or is this the end of Jerusalem as we know it? Even more, is this the last Jerusalem?

Navigating the dirt roads south of Bethlehem, the tires of my SUV grip the uneven terrain, finding their rhythm on the rugged path. I join Highway 60, a route that now pulses with life—an artery feeding the exodus. Cars pack the southbound lanes, and families in various states of panic flee toward uncertain safety. Northbound, the lanes are deserted, a grim sign that few are heading back. The road, once a simple two-lane highway, is now a chaotic stream of humanity and machinery, pushing southward in desperate waves. I fall in line behind a pickup, overloaded with furniture strapped haphazardly, mattresses bouncing on the wind. It's a convoy of fear.

With Bethlehem behind me, I'm swallowed by the contours of Judea, a land now more than a biblical name—a potential battleground in a new and terrifying conflict. The landscape changes, the hills rolling like waves, villages dotted here and there. Each kilometer feels like a journey backward in time through a history soaked in conflict.

Time blurs as I drive, and soon Hebron comes into view. Route 60 passes to the east of Hebron, and I imagine its ancient stone buildings standing resilient. Are the streets there like in Jerusalem? Skirting its eastern side, I press further south, the road growing quieter with each passing kilometer.

Just beyond Hebron, two figures materialize on the roadside, their silhouettes sharp against the barren landscape. Soldiers. Young. A man and a woman, armed and burdened with gear, their eyes scanning the horizon for hope. I pull over, my window on the rider's side rolling down.

"Where are you headed?" I ask in Hebrew.

"To Be'er Sheva," the young man responds. "The buses stopped running hours ago."

"Get in," I say.

They don't hesitate. They throw their gear into the back and hop inside, the young man—Oded—taking the passenger seat while the woman—Naomi—sits behind him. They are tense, their movements sharp, their eyes wary. The world outside feels ready to collapse.

We drive in silence at first, the road stretching out before us. Then Oded speaks, breaking the tension, "The country's mobilizing. And you?"

I hesitate, choosing my words carefully. "I'm not Israeli."

Oded turns slightly, surprised. "Your Hebrew is good."

"I've lived here fifteen years," I explain. "An archaeologist."

"And where are you going?" Naomi asks from the backseat, her voice soft but edged with steel.

"To the desert," I say.

Oded shakes his head slightly. "Dangerous. There's an army gathering across the Suez. North African countries, a coalition... they're watching us."

His words hang in the air. The desert I seek might soon be a battlefield. Israel's barrier along the southern border is strong— cameras, radars, steel fences—but it's not invincible. A determined enemy can punch through. We've seen that happen in the past, in Gaza. But I say nothing of my thoughts, just nod and keep driving.

We talk of war and politics, careful not to probe too deeply, knowing there are things we shouldn't share. They speak of troop movements, of alliances forming in the west and north, of the fog of war creeping in from every direction. I steer the conversation toward something else, something deeper.

"Do you believe God is still with you, the Jews?" I ask, keeping my tone neutral as if discussing the weather.

Naomi hesitates. "Our relationship with God . . . it's complicated. But we know the world will turn against us. We hope God will be with us in the end. We must believe that."

I meet her eyes in the rearview mirror. "I believe He is. Especially now."

There's silence, a beat too long, then Oded laughs—a nervous sound, out of place. "You sound like a prophet."

I chuckled. "Just an archaeologist, my friend."

We pull into a gas station near Be'er Sheva. There is a sign outside with a warning: 'No Gas.' But Oded and Naomi have a way. They go inside and speak with the owner, who comes out and fills my tank—kindness amid chaos and the authority of the military.

It is a three-hour drive from Be'er Sheva to Eilat, and I could easily have made it with the gas I had in my tank and full jerry cans as a backup. But having a full tank always gives comfort, especially when you don't know what lies ahead.

In Be'er Sheva, they direct me to a gathering point where Israeli troops are amassing. Before they leave, Oded warns me, his voice low and severe, "Avoid the main road to Eilat. It's a target. Missiles."

"Iron Dome isn't perfect," I finish for him.

He nods, his face grim. "The road to Eilat might be a death trap."

Then they are gone, swallowed by the preparations of war, and I'm alone again, my path leading southeast toward Eilat. Three hours of desolation stretch before me.

After fifteen minutes, the journey comes to an abrupt halt—cars backed up, a roadblock ahead. I step out, asking a man what's happened. "The bridge," he says flatly. "Blown. They're cutting us off."

I turn back, finding a dirt road I'd passed earlier, hoping it would lead me away from this entrapment. The hills are stark and quiet, and the world feels distant and foreign. Then, after ten minutes on the dirt road, I see something: a van in a ditch and something beside it that catches my eye.

I pull closer, and my breath hitches. Bodies. Two Israeli soldiers, lifeless on the ground. Weapons scattered like fallen leaves. I approach, dread coiling in my gut. They're not Oded and Naomi, but they were someone's children, someone's hope. I check for a pulse, already knowing the truth.

On the other side of the road, there is more horror, more bodies—civilian, it seems. Jeans and t-shirts, crumpled in death. A firefight. And no one survived.

I turn to leave, to get out of there as quickly as possible, my pulse pounding in my ears when a voice cuts through the stillness. "Stop." The word snaps like a whip.

I turn slowly, my hands instinctively rising. A woman steps around the van, an automatic rifle leveled at me. Her eyes are hard, her grip steady. Death, it seems, has not yet claimed everyone here.

Chapter 6

Staring down the muzzle of an automatic rifle, reality presses against my senses. The bodies sprawled around me are stark reminders of the consequences of this land. Survival hinges on not becoming one of them.

"Are you armed?" Her voice cuts through the air, sharp as glass.

"No weapons. Just a hunting knife in my car," I reply, stealing a glance at her and the lifeless figures on the ground. "What's happened here?"

"Lift your shirt and turn around." Her command is crisp, devoid of warmth.

I comply, baring my torso, my heart pounding in my throat.

"Now, get on the ground. Face down. Hands behind your head."

I kneel and then lower myself onto the dry earth, the gritty surface scraping against my cheek. The familiar scent of dust fills my nostrils—a smell tinged with the essence of history, the memory of countless winds sweeping over this barren land.

Will this be my last sensation? I can't shake the thought. The pressure of her weapon against my back is a cold reminder that cooperation is my only option.

Her hands trace my legs, a disconcerting examination. My instincts scream at me to grab her gun, but I know better. She's not an amateur, and the trigger is quicker than any reflex.

Finally, she withdraws the muzzle, allowing me to sit up, hands still atop my head.

"Why are you here?" Her voice is woven with suspicion.

"I was on my way to Eilat, but the bridges were destroyed, forcing me onto dirt roads," I explain, hoping to buy time.

"Why Eilat?"

"Not exactly Eilat, but nearby. I'm seeking safety away from Jerusalem."

"The desert's safety is an illusion," she retorts, her gaze sharp.

"Why do you say that?" Curiosity tinges on my voice.

"This." She gestures to the grim scene. "We were ambushed. My comrades are dead."

The two Israeli soldiers sprawled near me confirm her allegiance. "Ambushed by whom?" I ask, dread tightening my gut.

"I don't know. Stand up."

I rise cautiously, hands still atop my head.

"Search them. Their pockets," she orders, pointing to the bodies on the road. "Don't touch their weapons."

I lower my hands and approach the lifeless figures. Scattered rifles and handguns lie near them—each a grim reminder of their fate. My knowledge of firearms is limited to the M4A1 Carbine, standard for Israeli infantry. Once, during an archaeological dig, I'd fired at a tin can during target practice. I'd missed spectacularly.

The woman carries a shorter weapon than the M4A1, and I see a handgun holstered at her side.

The pockets yield papers and wallets, remnants of lives once full of stories. I've touched ancient bones that belonged to humans thousands of years ago, but to touch dead flesh is a new, unwelcome sensation. One set of keys jangles, hinting at an escape vehicle.

She watches, her gaze steady. "Papers, wallets. What do they reveal?"

"The first wallet has Israeli Shekels and another currency marked by the Central Bank of the Islamic Republic of Iran."

"I knew it." Her confirmation slices through the air like a bullet.

"Knew what?" I press.

"I had my suspicions," she replies.

"So, who are they?"

Her expression shifts, and the question hangs in the air. "What do I do with you now?" she asks, her voice a knife's blade.

"I could help get your van out of the ditch." I need her to see I'm no threat.

"No use. Bullets hit the tires and radiator. It's useless."

"They must have a car somewhere," I counter, revealing the keys I found.

"Let's find out. You walk ahead," she commands, the muzzle of her gun still trained on me.

We move past the bodies, the landscape a haunting reminder of our reality, and climb a dry hill, her presence a constant threat at my back.

Cresting the hill, a four-wheel drive appears.

"Go down and open the doors and trunk," she instructs, eyes scanning the surroundings.

I approach the vehicle slowly, hands visible. Inside, papers and food wrappings create a chaotic mess. In the trunk, a newspaper in Perso-Arabic script hints at the assailants' origins. My heart races as I rummage deeper and find boxes of ammunition and explosives.

"Take the boxes of ammo out and walk away," she orders, her voice precise and unwavering.

I grab six boxes of 9-millimeter full metal jacket bullets, each containing one hundred shells. As I walk fifteen steps away, she commands me to stop. "Now, sit."

I lower myself to the sandy floor, my eyes warily following her movements near the trunk.

She reaches into the back, and I struggle to see what she's doing. Then she hangs her rifle over her shoulder and steps toward me, unwinding a roll of blasting fuse. "Stand up and pick up the boxes," she says, and I obey.

"Follow me. Run."

I barely have time to process her command before she strikes a match, igniting the fuse. The thin, burning thread hisses with menace, a flicker of flame biting into the air.

With urgency, she bolts toward the summit of the dirt hill. I sprint behind her, adrenaline surging, trying to keep the boxes steady.

As we crest the hill, an explosion rocks the ground behind us and the earth trembles beneath my feet.

Chapter 7

Our lungs heave as we struggle to reclaim the breath we lost during our frantic sprint back to my car. She continues to look at me with a suspicious gaze. The echoes of the explosion still reverberate within me, my nerves vibrating in response to the shockwaves that rocked both the earth and my equilibrium.

I take a moment to look at her honestly. Age? Early thirties, perhaps, but it's hard to tell—Israeli women blend youthful liveliness with an uncanny wisdom. She's striking, but it's more than physical beauty. Strength is etched into every sinew, the compact grace of an athlete who navigates danger with steely resolve. She stands tall at about five feet nine, with piercing azure eyes, her dark hair securely pulled back in a ponytail. Practicality. European Ashkenazi heritage, maybe—an ancestral legacy of hardship and resilience that speaks volumes.

The absence of an Israeli uniform hints at her true affiliation—clandestine and elusive. Mossad, Shin Bet, or one of the other shadowy guardians of Israel's secrets. As she gazes at the bodies, a flicker of hesitation crosses her face, the first sign of vulnerability I've seen.

Rather than probe further into the ambush, I extend an offer of assistance. "How can I help? What do you want to do with your colleagues?"

Compassion bridges the gap between us, a silent understanding that transcends words. She inhales deeply, her breath heavy with sorrow. When she turns to look at me, a fleeting glimpse of sadness flickers in her gaze, a rare moment of honesty amid her steel façade. Losing comrades is like losing family; I can't imagine what she carries.

"It's not easy," I state, my voice softer. "Were they friends?"

"I didn't know them well," she replies, her voice steady but thick with emotion. "We met this morning, ordered to travel to an outpost together. But we were compatriots. It hurts."

"Shall we move them? They deserve a respectful farewell," I suggest gently, acknowledging the gravity of the situation.

"Yes," she breathes, determination mingling with grief. "Let's put them in the van, keep them safe from wild animals. I'll call for someone to retrieve them. Those four over there? Let them feed the wildlife."

I glance at the four ambushers, their hopes and dreams extinguished. "Are they Iranian?"

"Our intelligence identified Quds Force operatives in this area," she explains, her tone sharp. "They're the most secretive and powerful unit of the Iranian Revolutionary Guard. Trained for foreign operations, they report directly to the Supreme Leader of Iran. They're the ones who blew up our bridges. There's more than one group here."

That's the most she's said since I first encountered her. Without further words, pragmatism takes over, and we begin to move. Blood has dried on the wounds, a chaotic arrangement of gunfire to heads, chests, and legs. We gently transfer the two bodies to the van, a final act of kindness to shield them from the harsh environment.

Her eyes linger, a moment of sad reflection, a silent farewell to those she once shared a mission with. We roll the van's windows down a few inches, allowing for a breath of air.

She steps away, pulls out a cellphone from her pocket, and makes a call. The conversation is brief, and when she returns, relief softens her features. "Luckily, there was a signal. A team is on the way, but I need to move southeast, not far. Can you take me?"

For the first time, she requests rather than commands. "That's my direction. Yes, I can take you."

A tactical pause grants a fleeting moment of calm. She gathers her belongings—a travel bag that likely contains clothing and maybe a sleeping bag. We pay our silent respects to the fallen, and I watch her suppress emotion.

In the back of the van, I spot the two soldiers' travel bags, along with a pack of six one-liter bottles of water—no food. The urgency of their mission is apparent. They were racing to meet at an assigned location.

The weapons from the attackers and the soldiers, along with the six bottles, are piled atop my gear. She settles into the front seat, and I take the driver's position. Her words are clipped, terse: "Drive."

I fire up the engine, its roar breaking the silence as we leave behind the van and the grim remains of an enemy trap.

As we round the hill, we pass the smoldering wreckage of the shattered car—a haunting relic now. Images from the day cascade through my mind: mysterious blasts in Jerusalem, the fighter jet exploding overhead, the missile strike on the U.S. Embassy, and chaos in the streets. All against the backdrop of armies facing off.

This is far beyond the routine of an archaeologist accustomed to sifting through rocks and sand. I'm a detective of history, not trained to navigate between warring factions.

The world has shifted, and now I know more enemies are lurking in the shadows. As she said, the desert is not a safe place. The open road stretches ahead, but amidst the sparse conversation, an intense unease lingers in the air. Shadows dwell among these hills, hidden places where elusive adversaries may be waiting.

Chapter 8

We navigate the rugged terrain, miles from the main highway that stretches between Be'er Sheva and Eilat. On my dashboard, the GPS screen glows like a solitary blue dot, charting our course southward through a vast expanse of beige. The map reveals a patchwork of dirt roads, dried riverbeds, and rocky hills, the topography of an arid wilderness sprawling over five thousand square miles. The Negev, harsh yet hauntingly beautiful, boasts unique geological wonders—jagged hills, deep canyons, and resilient flora—all whispering the secrets of ancient civilizations scattered throughout its vastness.

Though I've dedicated months to excavations in the Negev, I've always avoided the searing summer heat and the freezing nights of January. Now, the memory of lifeless bodies and the fiery explosion lingers in my mind, the echoes reverberating as our vehicle bumps and sways over the relentless terrain. I can sense the turmoil coursing through my silent companion. Her mission, shrouded in secrecy, casts an uneasy shadow over our journey.

I know little about her—only that she needs transportation to an undisclosed location not far from here. It suits me; my destination lies deeper within the desert, away from the turmoil engulfing Israel. Once I've delivered her, I plan to head east toward Eilat. Five years ago, I stumbled upon an isolated cave hidden within a rocky outcrop in this wilderness—a secret spring tucked away in one of the countless wadis. There were no signs of human presence, no footprints or tire tracks to mar its tranquility.

As we traverse the barren landscape, her earlier warning about other Quds Force operatives in the area hangs in the air, a constant reminder of the prowling danger. Who knows what other hostile groups might be lurking in the shadows? It's a stark reality that belies the desert's deceptive calm.

To break the heavy silence, I attempt to initiate conversation. "I'm Thomas Thornton, but you can call me Tom. I'm an archaeologist—more specifically, Dr. Thomas Thornton."

"A doctor?" Her tone is cool.

"Yes, a doctor of archaeology," I reply, offering a reassuring smile, hoping to thaw the icy atmosphere.

Her directness doesn't waver as she probes, "How do you make a living doing that?"

A chuckle escapes me. "I receive my salary from a well-endowed foundation affiliated with an American university. For several months each year, I teach American students and lead them on excavations. I also give lectures at the Hebrew University of Jerusalem. Outside of that, I indulge in my passion—unearthing the mysteries of antiquity."

She glances my way before returning her focus to the road. "Not bad," she concedes.

"It has its moments," I reply, but my desire for mutual sharing lingers unfulfilled; she remains guarded.

"I've been working near the Western Wall in Jerusalem, collaborating with Dr. Schlomo Peretz and a team of Israeli archaeologists—until this morning, when we heard those explosions."

"Dr. Peretz?" Her interest is piqued.

"Yes, I've had the privilege of working alongside him on various significant sites over the years." He's a well-known figure in Israeli archaeology, so I thought the mention of his name might thaw her out a bit.

"How long have you been in Israel?"

"About fifteen years."

"Your Hebrew is competent."

"I learned it as a teenager while accompanying my grandfather on his summer trips here. He was also an archaeologist." I retrieve a small, framed photo from the glove compartment. "My grandfather and me at the Pool of Siloam."

She glances at it briefly before it disappears back into the compartment. "Are you married?" she inquires, straight forward.

I sigh, the wounds still fresh. "I was," I confess, the pain resurfacing. "My wife was also an archaeologist. She embarked on a short trip to Türkiye for a team excavating a Crusader site and met someone. She never returned to Israel." The heartache resurfaces like an old scar.

"Just like that?" Her tone is devoid of sympathy.

"He was the son of a billionaire, sweeping her off her feet with charm and lavish gifts. Now, she lives in a mansion in New York with a baby. Rumor has it her happiness isn't as enduring as she hoped."

"That might be for the best—for you. Where do you live?" The interrogation continues.

"I have a small house on the south side of Jerusalem, in a residential area. And you?"

"Near Tel Aviv," she replies, her answer vague—a deliberate choice to maintain secrecy. A testament to her training.

"May I ask your name?"

She relents, a small smile tugging at her lips. "My name is Ariela."

"Ariela, the lioness of God."

"Yes, I'm aware," she acknowledges, amusement flickering in her expression.

Time to confront the elephant in the car, to be as direct as an Israeli should be. "Do you work for Mossad or Shin Bet?"

Her surprise is palpable as she turns to face me. "I work with an organization that cooperates closely with the Israeli army."

"What's your mission?"

"To meet up with a team a few kilometers down the road."

"And what's their mission?"

"It's connected to the situation we're in."

"What do you mean? As your driver, don't you think I'm invested in our well-being, both yours and mine?"

"Did you hear about the explosions in Jerusalem this morning?"

"I was there. I heard them."

"They were car bombs. There are infiltrators in Israel, more than we initially realized. That's all I can say."

"I understand," I concede, respecting the boundaries of classified information. "The explosions triggered widespread panic, especially with news of large armies amassing in the north and east. I even picked up two hitchhikers in Hebron—two Israeli soldiers—who mentioned an army in the south."

"We're facing an unprecedented challenge."

"I know. This morning, I witnessed a fighter jet being shot down, and I was just outside the U.S. Embassy when a missile struck."

"The enemy jet was Russian, and the precision-guided missile aimed at the embassy was fired from Syria, bypassing our Iron Dome defense system."

"Where do you think this war is headed?" I can't help but seek her perspective.

Ariela inhales deeply, her words laden with gravity in the stifling confines of the car. "It's only going to get worse unless someone intervenes."

"That's how I see it too, and it just might happen," I recall the scriptures nestled in my backpack, regretting not delving deeper into their prophecies.

"I'm afraid we're on our own, but we will defend ourselves," she states firmly.

No time for a theological discussion. Instead, I ask, "How much farther are we going?"

Ariela consults the GPS map on her phone. "They should be about nine hundred meters ahead."

I continue driving steadily, veering around a hill and following the road south. Up ahead, I spot a crossing of two dirt roads, but no cars.

"No one is there," I remark.

"That's obvious. We're late by two hours; they must have moved on."

"Without you?"

"Our mission is important."

As we approach the crossroads, I halt the vehicle, step out, and signal for Ariela to do the same.

"What are you doing?" she asks.

"Get out." It's my turn to give orders now. "But stay behind me. I don't want our footprints to destroy the tracks."

I move slowly, scanning for car tracks. Near the crossroads, a flat, sandy area catches my eye. I stop, and Ariela joins me. "See there?" I point at the site. "Two cars were parked side by side. You can tell they rolled in here from the road we've been on. Then they departed southeast."

I follow the tracks twenty steps down the road to confirm my assumptions, and she follows.

"Are you certain?" she asks.

"Yes. Look, the same tracks of the two parked cars are going down this road."

"How do you know that?"

"I'm an archaeologist—an expert at deciphering the stories hiding in the earth." I offer a smile.

She reciprocates with a faint grin. "Are you planning to go in that direction?"

"Yes. As I said before, I have a destination in mind near Eilat."

"Can I hitch a ride?"

"You're more than welcome." I can't leave her out here on her own. Or to be realistic, it's more likely she would take my SUV and leave me here by myself.

We return to my car, the engine humming to life as we make the left turn at the crossroads, following the trail her comrades have set. It dawns on me that Ariela and I now share the same path as her comrades, which also means we share the same looming danger. Doubts flicker in my mind about venturing deeper into this space instead of returning to Be'er Sheva, but it's too late now.

Chapter 9

We press onward, navigating the weathered road, our eyes scanning the forsaken horizon for any sign of Ariela's team or the lurking Quds Force soldiers. Each mile echoes with the rapid shift in my reality—a stark reminder of how quickly life can pivot from the mundane to the chaotic.

I have been accustomed to a life of relative routine, my days primarily occupied with excavations beneath the earth's surface. Candidly speaking, I've deliberately avoided human relationships above ground. While I've explored the pages of God's book, it has often been as a historical text rather than a guiding force in my own life. Thus, in both the realms of human connections and spirituality, I have been lacking.

And yet, here I am, thrust into a chaotic world where I must navigate not only the physical danger around me but also the unfamiliar territory of depending on someone else for survival. Ariela, rifle poised and ready, is my only safeguard. Her presence evokes a mixture of comfort and shame. My survival now hinges on her skill with firearms, a reality that challenges every notion of masculinity I clung to. This is no trivial game of gender roles; it's a raw, brutal fight for survival, and my life may depend on her training.

The sun sinks lower in the sky, casting elongated shadows across the arid landscape. Ariela's colleagues seem to have disappeared, amplifying the solitude enveloping us. It becomes painfully clear that we must find shelter for the night.

After a brief, urgent discussion, I take charge, drawing on my familiarity with the desert. I spot an ancient riverbed, long, dry, and seemingly untouched by human hands. It snakes its way into the hills. I guide the car onto the riverbed, the rocky formations offering concealment.

"What's the plan?" Ariela's voice is steady but carries an edge of concern.

"Help me out here," I reply, my focus sharpening.

We exit the vehicle and retrace our steps to the dirt road. I gather some brush, snapping branches in two and handing a bundle to her. Together, we methodically erase our tracks, ensuring no sign of our presence remains. Gradually, it feels as though we've never been there at all.

With our traces concealed, we climb back into the car and continue along the rocky riverbed, winding around a hill until we reach a small gorge.

"This is where we'll spend the night," I declare, a note of finality in my voice.

"It looks promising," she responds. "We should hear any vehicles approaching, not that I think anyone will find us here. Those rocks can provide cover."

I retrieve her bag and gather my essentials—a sleeping bag, two liters of water, some food, utensils, and a small camping stove.

As I sort through our supplies, Ariela eyes the firearms we salvaged earlier. "Can you handle those?" she asks, a flicker of concern in her gaze.

"Not really," I admit. "I have only the basics down."

"You'll need to learn," she insists, handing me a loaded rifle, two clips, and a handgun with a holster. "Keep these close at all times."

Her hands deftly help me attach the holster to my belt, sliding the handgun into place. It's a strange weight, unfamiliar yet grounding. This moment signals a shift in our dynamic—her trust in me, however precarious, is now tangible.

We settle about fifty feet from the car, behind a large boulder that shields us from view, establishing our makeshift camp. I prepare a simple meal of instant rice and canned kosher meatballs, our appetites rekindled after a day steeped in stress. The silence enveloping us is heavy, broken only by the sounds of our meal, and I realize this is the first substantial food I've had since breakfast. Judging by Ariela's intense focus, she shares the same hunger.

Once we finish eating, I boil water for tea, serving it quietly as the night deepens around us. I reach into my bag and pull out a small chocolate bar, offering it to Ariela. "Here," I say, watching her expression.

She studies it for a moment, then smirks. "This is like dining in a gourmet restaurant."

"I wouldn't go that far," I reply, my thoughts drifting to the cities of Israel, wondering if they will ever again see the bustle of restaurants and laughter.

With our stomachs content, we unfurl our sleeping bags, the night sky above us unfurling in all its splendor, countless stars shimmering like distant beacons of hope. I kick off my shoes, peel off my pants and shirt, and settle into the warmth of my sleeping bag, my guns within arm's reach. I turn away as Ariela undresses, the rustle of fabric a reminder of our close quarters, the comforting presence of another human being amidst the world's chaos.

"This is spectacular," she observes, her gaze fixed on the sky.

I nod, my voice barely above a whisper. "I've spent many nights beneath these stars; it never ceases to amaze me."

"It makes you feel insignificant."

"It does. What we see above is just a fraction of the cosmos. We're mere specks—less than specks—in the grand scheme."

"But we possess intelligence, feelings, and life," she counters.

"According to your holy book," I say slowly, "we were created in God's image."

"That's what we're taught, but sometimes I wonder. There's so much greed and hatred."

"Referring to the Tanakh again, we've fallen from God's image, but we still bear His traits."

"I suppose you're right."

Silence wraps around us, a cocoon of contemplation as we stare into the depths of the universe. Finally, I venture into the heart of the conversation that lingers in the air. "Are you a religious person? Spiritual? Whatever you call it?"

"At times," Ariela replies, her tone thoughtful. "And you?"

"Yes, but after Debbie left me, I've slid into a routine devoid of deeper thought about God. Maybe it was anger or perhaps cowardice."

"I understand. Sometimes I'm angry at God, so I ignore Him."

"Do you think what's happening now might be prophetic?"

"What do you mean?"

"In the Tanakh, there are verses that speak of the end of the world as we know it. In Ezekiel, it's said that a terrible attack will befall Israel, leading God's people back to Him forever." I use the word Tanakh which is the Jewish term for the Old Testament.

"Where does it say that?"

"It's in Ezekiel, though I can't recall the exact chapter. I'm well-versed in the historical aspects of the Bible, Old and New Testaments—if I may use Christian terms. Still, I've never delved deeply into prophecy. But the Tanakh does foretell future events."

"That's more the domain of the Haredi, the ultra-Orthodox, with all their speculations. Still, I'd be interested to know what Ezekiel says."

"Perhaps tomorrow," I suggest, the night closing in.

"I'm curious," she admits. Then silence blankets us, exhaustion pulling at the edges of our conversation. She bids me goodnight. "*Laila Tov*, Doctor Tom." Her voice, a soothing melody in the dark, offers a hint of warmth amid the chaos.

"And to you, Ariela."

She turns onto her side, and I lie on my back, my eyes tracing constellations that flicker against the canvas of night. Today, the world has shifted beneath my feet, and I marvel at the sheer improbability of surviving this storm. My once-predictable life lies shattered, replaced by a wild existence hidden in the wilderness with a mysterious, formidable woman who captures my attention.

I ponder what the future holds, grateful for the warmth of my sleeping bag and the fragile illusion of safety, even as the darkness of ambiguity looms large.

Chapter 10

The first light of dawn creeps over the eastern horizon, a delicate line of gray heralding a new day. I've always enjoyed the stillness of early mornings, and despite the chaos that enveloped yesterday, I somehow found a fragment of peace in sleep. Lying still, I allow my mind to sift through the remnants of my thoughts. Sleep has a way of offering clarity, of mending the fractured pieces of life's intricate puzzle. But now, bathed in the sober light of dawn, reality settles heavily on my shoulders.

My mission remains unwavering—first, to help Ariela find her colleagues and then to the cave near Eilat. With that in mind, I quietly rise from my makeshift bed.

Ariela lies beside me, her face softened in slumber. She radiates an innocence that starkly contrasts with the turmoil surrounding us. Her tousled dark hair frames her face in wild abandon, illuminating her features in an almost angelic glow.

I slip away from our makeshift camp and approach my car, retrieving a thermos, a bottle of water, and a package of instant coffee. I set up the tiny camp stove, allowing the water to bubble and hiss. Once it's steaming, I mix the instant coffee into the thermos, crafting a modest brew to fortify us for the day ahead.

As the sun begins its ascent, Ariela stirs, her eyes immediately focused, as though instantly analyzing her surroundings. When she sees me, a soft smile breaks across her lips.

"*Boker Tov,*" I greet.

"*Boker Tov,*" she replies, her voice still thick with sleep.

"Did you sleep well?" I ask, curious about her rest.

"Yes, exhaustion has its rewards. How about you?"

"Likewise. Would you care for some breakfast?"

"*Bev akasha,*" she replies, which in Hebrew means please.

I return to my car, rummaging through supplies for instant oatmeal, hesitating momentarily to grant her the privacy she deserves as she changes. As I prepare the oatmeal, adding hot water and stirring until it becomes a mushy consistency, nostalgia washes over me. The memories of vibrant Israeli breakfasts flood my mind: fluffy pita bread, creamy cheeses, fresh salads, smoky fish, and sweet fruits—all the flavors of life now feel like distant echoes.

Once the oatmeal is ready, I hand her a bowl and take one for myself.

"It's not exactly an Israeli breakfast," I remark with a chuckle, "but it should keep us going."

"Thank you," she says gratefully. "Without you, I'd likely be hungry right now."

After finishing our meal, I pour two steaming cups of coffee, handing one to her while keeping the other. We sit on our sleeping bags, soaking in the warmth of the morning sun.

"Any thoughts on our plans for the day?" I ask, breaking the silence.

Ariela's brow furrows in contemplation. "I need to find my team. They headed east, the same way we are going. So, let's continue."

"Sounds good to me."

"There's something that worries me," she confides, her voice low. "You mentioned your lack of shooting skills. That could be a problem if we encounter trouble. I think it's essential for you to receive some basic training—enough to give you confidence."

I pause to absorb her suggestion. Firearms have always seemed like instruments for the military, tools of violence I never envisioned myself using. Yet, her point rings true. In a life-or-death scenario, cowering in a corner is not an option. "Yes, how do we proceed?" I agree.

"There's a deeper section of this wadi that would serve perfectly for practice. The walls will muffle the sound of gunfire, and we're far from the main road."

"Alright, let's do it."

We gather our rifles, handguns, and a box of ammunition and head deeper into the wadi. Ariela retrieves the empty can from last night and places it against the wadi wall, then leads me to a spot about twenty paces away.

Taking her time, she explains the various components of the rifle, the safety switch, how to change the clip, and the distinctions between single and automatic firing modes. "Now, go ahead and shoot at the can."

With a steady hand, I raise the rifle and aim, squeezing the trigger. The shot rings out, surprisingly closer to the target than I anticipated.

"*Tov*," she praises, a flicker of approval in her eyes. "Now, shoot again—slowly."

I follow her instructions, pulling the trigger with intention, each shot echoing through the wadi. As I empty the clip, I feel a strange sense of empowerment with each successive hit.

Setting the rifle aside, Ariela turns her attention to the handgun, guiding me through its mechanics. "Hopefully, we won't need to use these," she states, "but we must be prepared."

It's a sentiment that resonates deeply within me—the ever-present Israeli mindset of readiness. While this practice doesn't transform me into an expert, it instills a sense of familiarity that I sorely lacked. I've graduated from a complete novice to a hazardous entry-level shooter.

Once our training concludes, we return to the car, our determination to press east unwavering. After stowing our gear, I start the engine, and we drive down the riverbed, rejoining the dirt road that stretches ahead.

Ariela gazes forward, her rifle resting beside her. "You mentioned a verse from the Tanakh about God watching over Israel. Do you remember it?"

I chuckle softly. "I'm afraid that got lost in the morning shuffle of breakfast and practice."

"I want to know that verse," she insists. "I'm deeply concerned for my country, and you mentioned prophecies. What do they reveal?"

It's clear she embodies the spirit of a secular Israeli. I halt the car and reach into my backpack, retrieving my worn, small-print Bible. The pages, especially those detailing historical narratives, bear the marks of countless readings. Flipping through the familiar passages, I finally locate the book of Ezekiel.

"Here it is," I announce, excitement lacing my voice. "In Ezekiel chapter 38, it states: *'This is what will happen in that day: When Gog attacks the land of Israel, my hot anger will be aroused, declares the Sovereign Lord.' It goes on to describe God sending fire upon Gog and Magog, among other things.*"

Ariela's expression shifts; a spark of hope dances in her eyes. "So, God has not abandoned us, as I feared."

"Not according to this," I affirm, the words solidifying in the air between us.

"What are Gog and Magog?" she asks, a hint of curiosity threading through her voice.

"Ah, this is where my background in archaeology comes into play. Many historians believe they symbolize modern-day Russia."

"And Russia is one of the nations that are hostile to us," she replies, her tone grave.

"Exactly," I confirm, "and these verses outline other nations gathering on Israel's borders."

"Isn't it strange that this was predicted thousands of years ago?" she muses.

"I share that wonder. Yet here we are, living through what was foretold. The realm of the unseen seems ever more relevant. Like you, I've overlooked it, but perhaps it's time we take it more seriously."

"What you read is comforting," she reflects, her tone thoughtful. "I wish it were true."

"Do you have doubts?" I probe gently.

"I know I shouldn't," she admits.

"All we can do is hope and trust. One thing I've discovered as an archaeologist is the Bible's remarkable accuracy as a historical document. The more we dig, the more we find—places, people, events—all aligning with its narratives. If that's the case, why not consider that its prophecies might hold truth as well?"

"It does provide a glimmer of hope," she concedes.

"Indeed, and as we hope, let's concentrate on surviving today," I urge, shifting our focus back to the present.

"I agree," Ariela affirms. "I want to learn more, but first, I must find my team."

Turning the ignition, the engine roars to life once more, propelling us forward into the unfamiliar. The road stretches ahead, winding into the uncertain future. We are two souls bound by divergent quests: one to find a team bent on eliminating terror, the other seeking solace in this desolate expanse. Yet, those verses from Ezekiel open a broader panorama that transcends mere survival.

Somewhere in the depths of my heart, I sense an undeniable spiritual undercurrent guiding our journey. This ethereal purpose may not only shape our actions but also serve as the key to our very survival.

Chapter 11

The gravity of our situation bears down on me. What should have been a mere two-hour drive along a paved highway has transformed into an arduous odyssey of eight to ten hours on treacherous dirt roads. My rugged SUV strains against the uneven terrain, a beast of burden in this desolate wasteland. I dare not push it too hard; the last thing we need is to damage the vehicle and become stranded, vulnerable to whatever dangers lurk in this rugged landscape.

I break the silence, my voice taut with unease. "Maybe we should reconsider and head back to the main highway. There, you might be able to get a phone signal, and your organization could help us locate your team."

Ariela gazes ahead at the formidable craggy mountains looming ominously in our path. Her eyes reflect a blend of apprehension as she weighs my suggestion. "That might be a wise choice. These hills make us sitting ducks. Is there a town nearby?"

I glance at the GPS screen. "Yes, there's a town called Mitzpe Ramon about ten kilometers from here."

"Let's go," she affirms, her tone resolute. "Tell me, what do you know about this town?"

As a member of Israeli intelligence, she probably knows a lot about this town. She is testing me. I answer, "I've passed by it a few times and even stopped there once. I believe it was founded in the '50s, initially as a military outpost or a camp for workers constructing the road to Eilat. The population might be around two thousand, or maybe more."

Ariela absorbs this information. I suspect she hasn't revealed the full extent of what's at stake here.

The landscape around us unfolds, the harsh beauty of the Negev starkly contrasting with the chaos we've left behind. After driving a couple of kilometers, I steer onto a crossroads, turning north and winding through the craggy mountains that dominate our surroundings. The sun blazes overhead, casting long shadows across the earth. I steal a glance at Ariela; her vigilance is evident.

"The road's rough," I note, my grip on the steering wheel tightening involuntarily.

She nods, determined steadfast. "Proceed with caution. This place conceals more than just natural wonders."

The car's suspension groans with each jolt, a mechanical protest that mirrors my unease. My gaze shifts to the rocky formations that could harbor lurking threats. The Negev, with its raw beauty, is a double-edged sword, hiding dangers beneath its stark surface. With the war escalating to the north, this isolated region has become a haven for both those seeking refuge and those intent on sowing chaos.

After a hard bump into a pothole, Ariela turns to me. "We can't afford a breakdown," she emphasizes, her voice steady.

I nod, my knuckles white from gripping the steering wheel. She's right; being stranded here is a chilling thought that we dare not entertain. I can't help but glance at the rearview mirror, scanning for any signs of pursuit, any hint of danger lurking in our wake.

We emerge from the constricted confines of a narrow canyon into a barren expanse, and the sight that greets us is anything but reassuring. A car, half off the road with its front tire buried in sand, stands as a testament to misfortune. A man is crouched low, digging around the tire. I sense Ariela's distrust.

"Be careful," she states.

My foot eases off the accelerator as I guide the car to a halt, stopping about fifty meters from the stranded vehicle.

Ariela swings her door open, her rifle concealed behind the car door. Her voice carries authority tinged with caution as she addresses the man. "What happened?"

He straightens up, sand clinging to his hands, his face a mask of frustration. "I got stuck," he replies brusquely.

Though his words are in Hebrew, an unsettling foreign accent punctuates them. Ariela remains vigilant, her guard unwavering as she instructs me with steely resolve.

"Stay here and keep the motor running."

As she steps out, rifle in hand, her focus is trained on the man before her. The man's nerves fray as he suddenly abandons his façade of helplessness. In a swift and alarming motion, he flings himself around the car, brandishing a rifle. Bullets erupt from his weapon, zinging haphazardly above us. Panic surges through me, and I instinctively hunch down in my seat.

But Ariela reacts faster. Her rifle springs to her shoulder, and with unwavering precision, she fires a single shot. The man crumples backward, his threat extinguished in an instant, his lifeless body falling onto the sand.

Ariela retakes her position behind the open door, surveying the terrain on the right side of the car. "Get your rifle and keep watch on the other side."

I take my rifle, open my door, and stand on the ground, mirroring her stance. The hills lie silent, yet we remain motionless, hearts pounding. Ariela's watchful eyes sweep the landscape. I do my best to mirror her caution.

Then, a realization strikes me: my training as an archaeologist is surprisingly relevant today. An archaeologist must be attuned to geology, recognizing the strata of hills and the types of rocks, whether in their natural state or utilized in human constructions. I find myself scanning the hills, instinctively sensing whether architectural structures lie hidden beneath them. Today, that attention to detail feels crucial. I see no movement; everything appears natural, in its rightful place.

Finally, Ariela's voice breaks the stillness, tinged with intrigue and trepidation. "It's strange that he was out here alone. I wonder why."

Nervous, I respond, "Do you have any idea how many terrorists might be lurking around here?"

Her seriousness deepens. "Our intelligence suggested at least twenty, possibly more. We suspect someone helped them enter the country and continues to assist them."

My mind races with possibilities. "Could they be tracked from above, with satellites or drones?"

Ariela's response is tempered by the harsh realities of this terrain. "It's not that simple. The Negev might look barren, but it's riddled with small settlements—Bedouins, Arabs, Palestinians, Christians, and, of course, Jews. These terrorists can blend in, using individual cars instead of a convoy. They know how to disappear into the landscape."

The mystery deepens as I inquire about the fallen man. "So, who was he?"

Ariela's gaze remains fixed on the horizon. "He could be an accomplice or one of them. His Hebrew had an Iranian accent, suggesting ties to terrorism, but his solitary presence raises questions. And his shots were poorly aimed; he wasn't well-trained. Perhaps he got stuck here when he was supposed to be better positioned on a hill, keeping watch."

"Get back in the car, drive forward slowly, but stay in the vehicle and keep the engine running," she instructs.

I comply, inching the car closer to the abandoned vehicle, vigilant and ready as she walks, taking cover behind the door. When we reach the man's car, I come to a stop and wait for Ariela as she cautiously circles it, looking inside.

She returns, clutching the man's rifle and taking a seat beside me. Her words hang heavy in the air. "There's nothing in the car, no identification in the glove compartment, nor on him. It's a mystery. Let's get out of here."

As I engage the gears and accelerate, my thoughts swirl with images of the fallen man. The sight of life extinguished so abruptly unsettles me, and I struggle to find the right words.

"Are you okay?" I finally manage to ask.

Ariela takes a deep breath, her gaze unwavering from the terrain ahead. "It's never easy, but he fired first. It was self-defense."

I nod, the horror of our situation evident.

We drive away, and with each kilometer that passes, we draw closer to Mitzpe Ramon, the town looming like a distant hope on the horizon.

Chapter 12

As we approach Mitzpe Ramon, the entrance to the town is flanked by two weary Israeli soldiers. Their expressions reflect the heavy burden of watchfulness they carry in these uncertain times.

Before we close the distance to these guardians, Ariela, her eyes flickering with a blend of caution, instructs me to halt the car. "Our vehicle is loaded with weapons. I need to speak with them," she says urgently.

Leaving her rifle and handgun behind, she steps out of the SUV, raising her hands in a gesture of surrender. Every step toward the soldiers is measured.

The soldiers train their weapons on her as a tense exchange begins, their hushed voices blending into a background of ominous quiet. I strain to catch snippets of their conversation, but I can only grasp fragmented words.

After what feels like an eternity, Ariela signals for me to advance. The soldiers lower their weapons, allowing us to pass, and they direct us toward the town's heart.

Mitzpe Ramon unfolds before us like a ghost town, its buildings standing silent. It feels as if most of the population has vanished. We pull up in front of a modern structure marked "Mitzpe Ramon Community Center." I park the SUV, and we step inside. The building is spacious, featuring a large auditorium, a sports hall, a library, and a cafeteria.

Inside the entrance area, an Israeli army officer is deep in conversation with two elderly men, their faces filled with worry. Ariela introduces herself and requests a private meeting with the officer.

As they withdraw into a nearby room, I engage the two men in conversation. One of them, the mayor, listens intently as I recount our harrowing encounter with the terrorists. Their expressions darken as the gravity of our situation sinks in.

"It's a grim reality here," the mayor tells me, his voice heavy with concern. "Attacks on crucial infrastructure have crippled the region. Bridges, buildings, and communication towers have been reduced to rubble. Telecommunications from Be'er Sheva to Eilat have been severed, and the main fiber optic line is obliterated.

This devastation was calculated and deliberate, planned over time."

I nod, absorbing his words. "People are working hard to restore roads and communications, but it may take days," he adds, his brow furrowing with worry.

Electricity in the town is supplied by a generator. Yet amidst the chaos, a lone survivalist operates a makeshift radio station, its feeble signals reaching out into the fractured world.

With a citizen's band radio, this radio operator can communicate with army headquarters in Tel Aviv, where the Israel Defense Forces, the Ministry of Defense, and intelligence agencies are headquartered.

"The foreign troops haven't yet set foot on Israeli soil," the mayor continues, "but their presence looms ominously. Skirmishes involving fighter jets have become unsettlingly common. Missiles and drones have been intercepted at our borders, causing minor damage so far, except for the U.S. Embassy. Terror attacks have erupted across the nation, fueling anxiety within the population."

As I ponder our presence here, a nagging question haunts me. Is this the right course of action for me? Is fleeing to the mountains, as the verse suggests, truly the extent of my purpose? Could there be a role for me beyond mere survival, one that might impact the unfolding events? It feels cowardly to only look out for myself.

Ariela reappears with the officer, her face set in a mask of determination. Though I can't discern the details of their discussion, I'm eager to hear her next words. Speaking to the mayor, she requests the use of the citizen's band radio to contact her command center—likely a specialized organization linked to the Ministry of Defense.

She's escorted to a room, and as she establishes contact, I step outside. For the first time in a long while, I feel compelled to pray. "God, amidst all this chaos, reveal if there's a purpose for me in this turmoil. And please protect your people."

A sense of calm washes over me after the prayer, but no celestial signs emerge to guide my path.

When I return to the community hall, Ariela is there, her expression serious. "The bridges between here and Eilat have been destroyed," she informs me, "but there are alternative routes. If you take the highway, you could reach Eilat in a couple of hours."

"Thank you for the information," I reply, my thoughts racing. "And what about you?"

She reveals her mission—a dangerous assignment that takes her toward an encampment of Quds Force soldiers, possibly embedded in a Bedouin camp. Her team is hidden in the hills nearby, awaiting reinforcements, and her orders are clear: she must join them.

"How will you get there?" I ask, concern creeping into my voice.

"That's the challenge," she admits. "I can wait for an army vehicle coming from Be'er Sheva in two hours, or I can explore alternatives."

For a moment, I weigh my options. My objective has been to find isolation in the mountains near Eilat to escape the brewing storm. Is that selfish? Ariela's mission could save countless lives, while mine feels like mere self-preservation. Does she need assistance? An unexpected role beckons—a chance to be her chauffeur on a treacherous journey. At the very least, I could help her reach her destination.

"Can I take you?" I offer, a sense of purpose igniting within me. Perhaps this is the path God has carved for me amidst the chaos.

Chapter 13

Deciding to assist Ariela on her mission feels like leaping into the abyss. The mayor, his expression grave with concern, lead us to a back room in the community hall, where he gives us ten kilos of dates and ten kilos of dried figs—the age-old sustenance of desert travelers. It is a silent acknowledgment of the arduous journey that lies ahead.

Back in the car, we drive away from Mitzpe Ramon, following the asphalt road southward. The route winds down a long curve, descending five hundred meters into the depths of the Makhtesh Ramon crater—an impressive geological formation sculpted by erosion rather than volcanic or meteoric forces. This box canyon stretches forty kilometers long and reaches widths of up to ten kilometers, its steep walls a testament to nature's artistry.

After traversing the crater, we ascend the opposite side, and then turn onto a dirt road that veers further south. The decision to take this route feels peculiar, a deliberate choice against the more straightforward path to Eilat. Did I make the right choice by agreeing to help Ariela reach her destination?

Ariela has marked the meeting point on both the GPS screen on my dashboard and her phone's map. We need to drive about sixteen kilometers on this road—roughly ten miles.

With Ariela beside me, we navigate the twisting road that winds through the rugged Negev landscape. The raw beauty of the terrain stands in stark contrast to the ever-present reality of war and Ariela's mission. I steal glances at the weapons stacked in the back of my car, a formidable arsenal we could have left behind in Mitzpe Ramon but chose to carry.

Ariela's gaze remains locked on the road ahead as she begins to unfold the details of her mission, her tone serious. "The Quds Force soldiers are rumored to be hiding within a Bedouin encampment. They are among the most highly trained in the Iranian Revolutionary Guard. We aren't sure if the Bedouins are accomplices or hostages, so we must proceed with utmost caution."

"Why is that?" I ask, the complexity of the mission starting to dawn on me.

"Many Bedouins serve in the Israeli army. They are fellow Israelis. If we storm that encampment with guns blazing, innocent lives could be lost, and we can't allow that. We risk losing the support of that community as well."

"Is there a way to isolate the Quds Force group from the encampment, maybe neutralize them with a missile strike?" I press further.

She contemplates for a moment. "There's a drone surveilling the camp. If the terrorists make a move, we can engage, but there's a risk they may have Bedouin hostages in their vehicles."

"What's the plan then?"

"My team awaits further orders," she replies, her voice hinting at the intricate nature of their mission.

"Why do they need you on-site?" I ask, sensing her openness to discuss tactics.

Ariela offers a cryptic response. "The more fighters we have, the stronger our position."

"Are you a leader in your group?" I recall the deference shown to her by both the army officer and the mayor of Mitzpe Ramon.

She sidesteps the question. "I'm part of the chain of command, but in these operations, hierarchy takes a back seat. We act as a cohesive team."

The ambiguity in her words gnaws at me, but it's evident she holds a crucial role. As the miles stretch on, the weight of our impending destination looms like an approaching storm.

As we navigate the bumpy road, we receive sporadic updates from the makeshift desert radio station. The voice crackling over the airwaves connects us to the world left behind in Mitzpe Ramon, relaying the escalating turmoil in the north. Foreign armies advance toward Israel's borders, primarily from Syria. The skies above have become a battleground, with missiles fired from southern Lebanon met by Israel's Iron Dome defenses. Israeli aircraft retaliated with pinpoint strikes against the positions from which the rockets were launched.

As the sun inches toward the horizon, we finally reach the designated meeting point with Ariela's team—a valley where rocky outcrops provide concealment and refuge. Ariela signals me to park near four military vehicles, where a man holding a rifle stands guard. She waves at him, smiling.

"This camp is hidden from prying eyes," she quickly explains. "There's a mountain between us and the Bedouin village, and we're far enough away so they can't hear the car."

I wait in the car while Ariela approaches the guard, clearly at ease with him. After a brief exchange, she motions for me to join her, and I step into the warmth of the afternoon.

As we move toward her concealed team, the gravity of the situation becomes evident. Twelve elite soldiers stand bathed in the afternoon light, their imposing presence contrasting sharply with the stark, rocky backdrop of the Negev. They form a unified front, their expressions revealing the gravity of their mission.

They greet Ariela with smiles, but their eyes shift to me with suspicion. "He's okay," she assures them, and that's all it takes for them to relax.

Their attire is carefully chosen to blend into the harsh terrain. Each person wears earth-toned camouflage that melds seamlessly with the natural hues of sand and stone.

Their rifles and small backpacks are neatly arranged in the shade near a rock. Tactical vests strapped to their torsos carry an assortment of ammunition, grenades, and communication devices. Holstered pistols, flashbangs, and utility tools adorn their belts, ready to be deployed at a moment's notice.

Among this formidable team, three women stand tall, their presence a testament to their courage. Dressed simply, they command the same respect as their male counterparts. Their faces reflect a steely resolve, an unspoken promise to fulfill their mission at any cost. Young and attractive, they possess an aura that suggests they should not be underestimated.

The nine men look seasoned, some wearing meticulously groomed beards while others have more rugged appearances.

Surrounding them, the rocky outcrops provide both shelter and a vantage point—a strategic choice made by the team to maintain the element of surprise.

Ariela breaks away from me, huddling with her team members in whispered conversations, sharing critical updates. I can only imagine the intricacies of their mission as they gather around a map, strategizing.

When she returns to me, Ariela whispers urgently, "You must go." As her team prepares to move out, she walks me to my car. Standing close, her expression a blend of gratitude and concern, she says, "You've been a crucial part of this," her voice low yet resolute.

As she retrieves her bag from my car, I say, "Good luck."

"Thank you," she replies.

Noticing the pile of rifles and guns we collected, I ask, "What should we do with these?"

"Keep them. You never know what lies ahead or whom you might encounter who may need them."

It's an awkward moment to say goodbye to someone with whom I've shared such an extraordinary experience. We've forged a connection through shared danger, and beneath it all, I feel an overwhelming desire to remain by her side, but I know that's impossible.

PDF CONTAINS ICC COLOR PROFILES: We request files with no color profiles assigned. Please convert all colors to grayscale for black and white images, or CMYK for color images and remove all color profiles. Saving a new PDF with the default setting of PDF/X-1a:2001 will address the issue. For best results, please correct the issue(s) listed. You may refer to the File Creation Guide for further instructions on creating a compliant PDF. "Stay vigilant and stay safe," she advises. "Our paths may cross again, hopefully under better circumstances. And thank you, Dr. Tom." With that, she moves closer, offering a quick but meaningful hug before turning away with determination.

As she rejoins her team, they gather their weapons and gear. Four of them begin their ascent of the hill, seamlessly merging with the landscape, while the others disperse into the four military vehicles. They turn onto the dirt road, heading left, and I assume they'll position themselves around the Bedouin encampment.

Now, alone in this vast expanse, I start the car and turn right onto the dirt road, going in the opposite direction of Ariela's team.

With the sun low in the sky, I won't go far. I need to find a secluded place to spend the night.

Chapter 14

As I leave Ariela and her team behind, the winding road into the hills unfurls like an unfamiliar story, each curve triggering memories of the days' past. Solitude settles around me, heavy yet oddly comforting.

Relief washes over me knowing that the Quds Force operatives are now within the Bedouin encampment, awaiting justice from the Israeli Shin Bet team. My thoughts drift to Shin Bet, Israel's internal security agency, renowned for its covert operations to dismantle terrorist networks. With its motto, "Shield and not seen," they operate under the Prime Minister's direct authority, their methods shrouded in secrecy. Who else could Ariela be working with? I can't shake the worry for her safety, offering a silent prayer as I navigate the empty road.

Thoughts of Zevi Yitzhak, the new Prime Minister, flutter through my mind. How can he focus on the Shin Bet operation in the Negev with so many pressing issues at hand? The solitude allows my mind to wander, and I find myself reflecting on the time spent with Ariela—a unique blend of camaraderie and danger. The quiet of the desert only amplifies my longing for her presence.

I reach for the car radio, grateful for the connection to the outside world. The voice from the makeshift desert station in Mitzpe Ramon cuts through the stillness, reporting on the escalating war. Each word tightens the knot in my stomach. Foreign armies advance toward Israel's borders, missiles exchanged like grim greetings between opposing forces. The sheer scale of the threat looms large, a reminder of the fragility of our existence.

As I drive, my thoughts meander into the spiritual implications of these dire signs. I recall our discussions about Ezekiel and the prophetic verses that seem eerily relevant. "This is what the Sovereign Lord says: I am against you, Gog," echoes in my mind as I contemplate the unfolding chaos. I resolve to revisit those chapters, eager for deeper understanding.

The road twists into the mountains, rugged peaks standing sentinel against the darkening sky. I envision my intended destination, a hidden cave not far from Eilat. It offers seclusion and a reliable water source—an oasis amid turmoil. I remember other potential sanctuaries discovered during archaeological expeditions; sites that could serve as backups should the cave prove uninhabitable. The historic site of Petra, just across the border in Jordan, offers possibilities, but I hope it won't come to that.

Three miles from parting with Ariela, I find a suitable canyon to set up camp. Hidden from view, I bring the car to a halt and begin to prepare a basic campsite. With my camp stove, I heat water and prepare an instant meal, savoring the small comfort it provides. Selecting a concealed spot away from the car for safety, I unfurl my sleeping bag, positioning my rifle and handgun within easy reach.

As daylight fades, I settle against a sturdy rock, retrieving a small Bible from my backpack. The verses from Ezekiel that Ariela had shown interest in spark my curiosity, so I read aloud from Chapter 38, tracing the prophecies outlined in the Book of Daniel. The windswept landscape seems to echo the ancient words, each syllable resonating with the present turmoil and the promise of divine intervention.

Ezekiel and Daniel, once mere historical texts, now feel like pieces of an unfolding prophetic puzzle. Both speak of a formidable leader, Gog, and the King of the North—a power-hungry figure intent on challenging divine authority. Nations like Persia, Cush, Put, Gomer, and Beth Togarmah march against Israel, mirroring the geopolitical tensions of today with Iran, Sudan, Libya, Türkiye, and perhaps part of Ethiopia. Other African nations are likely to join this coalition.

The timing of this impending invasion is unequivocal. Ezekiel speaks of events "in the last days," while Daniel adds that it will occur "at the time of the end." The reunification of Judea and Samaria and the return of the dispersed children of Abraham only lend credence to these ancient prophecies.

The motives of these nations are glaringly apparent. Gog seeks to plunder Israel, stripping it of its wealth. Daniel's narrative echoes this ambition, portraying the King of the North as he covets Israel's lands and riches. Israel's natural gas reserves, technological prowess, and agricultural bounty make it an irresistible target, and its significance is revealed in the prophets' words that label it "the center of the world."

Yet, it is the apocalyptic climax of these prophecies that resonates most profoundly within me. In both Ezekiel and Daniel, the invaders ultimately face divine wrath. A storm of fire, pestilence, and earthquakes herald their destruction. Ezekiel even prophesies that the invading armies will turn on each other, thereby demonstrating God's omnipotent presence. In that moment, all will recognize the power of the Almighty.

As I gaze upon the stark beauty of the Negev, these thoughts swirl around me, a reminder of the profound commitment from a higher power to the fate of Israel. The reality of these ancient texts has transformed from an academic pursuit to a frightening truth unfolding before my eyes, yet within the fear lies a sense of reassurance.

Oddly, as a Christian, I find my knowledge of the Old Testament outweighs that of the New Testament, thanks to my archaeological experiences. This leads me to consider the Book of Revelation—a cryptic text I've grappled with in the past. How does it intertwine with the prophecies of Ezekiel and Daniel? My thirst for understanding deepens, but time is a luxury I cannot afford.

Night descends, wrapping the desert in darkness. I could use a flashlight, but in the stillness of the desert, lights can be seen from great distances. Tucking the Bible back into my backpack, I prepare for sleep, nestling into my sleeping bag with my rifle and handgun nearby.

Underneath a canopy of stars, the solitude eats at my soul. I feel vulnerable, not only from the pressing danger. My time with Ariela, while fraught with danger, somehow imbued my journey with purpose. But it is more than that. I've been lonely, and she filled a need for companionship. A remarkable woman like that leaves an imprint, one that attracts me. I wish I could be with her more, but I know it is not possible. Maybe I should be resigned to a sad, pitiful existence as a recluse.

Finally, sleep claims me.

The first light of dawn awakens me, the harsh sun piercing through the stillness. As I rise, the earth trembles beneath me. It's another earthquake. I take a deep breath and dress, the mountains looming before me, reminding me of the rugged path I've chosen.

After a breakfast of oatmeal mixed with a date and dried fig, I break camp and return to my car. Switching on the radio, I listen to reports of the ongoing conflict. Israel stands resilient, yet the foreign armies press forward. The world hangs in the balance, and I'm left contemplating my place in this unfolding drama.

Sitting in my car, I feel the signs of the last days converging around me, an overwhelming sensation of being part of something far greater than myself. As I start the car and merge back onto the road, I question my destination. Which way should I turn?

Chapter 15

Curiosity has always been a double-edged sword for me, propelling me into the heart of ancient mysteries and hidden truths. Today, it steers me down an unexpected path. Instead of heading straight to Eilat, I find myself turning back, driven by a need to uncover the events at the Bedouin camp. I can't shake the thought—what happened during the confrontation between Shin Bet and the Quds Force? And most importantly, is Ariela safe?

As I retrace my route toward the Shin Bet's former position, I park my SUV hastily, grabbing my binoculars and a water bottle before setting off. With purposeful strides, I ascend a nearby hill, seeking refuge in the shade of a massive rock. Camouflaged and alert, I crouch low, honing my senses as I prepare to survey the encampment below.

The scene before me is far from what I anticipated—just three tents nestled within an out-of-the-way stretch of hills. Though Bedouins have historically roamed the deserts with their camels, many now lead more settled lives, engaging in trade and various jobs. The image of wandering nomads has faded, although today, some still preserve their rich heritage through poetry, music, and traditional crafts.

Below me lies a trio of tents woven from earthy fabrics adorned with intricate geometric patterns that hint at the Bedouins' vibrant culture. A pickup truck sits parked nearby, while a small fire pit at the center sends up a thin plume of smoke. Four goats graze on the sparse sagebrush, adding life to the otherwise quiet scene.

What unfolds beneath me occurs with an unsettling calmness. A young girl emerges from one of the tents, speaking to the goats as if they were friends. Moments later, two women appear, their brightly colored dresses contrasting sharply with the muted landscape. They gather around the fire pit, one pouring water into a pot and hanging it over the flames, perhaps to brew tea.

Yet, the absence of men and any signs of conflict fill me with unease. The silence is oppressive, and my mind races with questions. What transpired in the hours since my departure?

Where are the Quds Force operatives? And what of the elusive Israeli team?

My thoughts drift to Ariela, the brave operative whose fate feels shrouded in mystery. I long to descend into the village, to seek answers, but caution anchors me. Recent brushes with danger have left me wary.

With more questions than clarity, I decide to retreat to my vehicle—my temporary sanctuary. Perhaps some distance will lend me a clearer perspective. However, as I approach my car, dread washes over me like ice water.

A weathered pickup truck is parked next to my SUV, and two men stand nearby. They embody a blend of ancient tradition and modern practicality, their heads wrapped in traditional Bedouin keffiyeh yet dressed in t-shirts and jeans. Their curious gazes are fixed on my vehicle, and I realize with a jolt that my handgun and rifle lie exposed inside. The arsenal of weapons in the back is covered.

Panic surges through me as I consider the implications. Are they allies or adversaries? The men remain oblivious to my presence until I inadvertently kick a small rock, the noise echoing in the stillness. Their heads snap in my direction, and I can't tell if they're armed. Bedouin men often carry knives, and I might be stepping into dangerous territory.

In this tense moment, with Ariela's fate and the mysteries of the Bedouin village hanging in the balance, I must assess whether they pose a threat.

I muster my courage and greet them in Arabic, saying, "*As-salaam alaikum*," a traditional way to wish peace upon others. The two men exchange surprised glances. It's uncommon for a Westerner to greet them in their language. The taller one responds, "*Wa-alaikum as-salaam*," a sign of mutual respect.

The smaller man, still eyeing me curiously, says in Arabic, "You speak our language."

"Yes," I reply. "I am an archaeologist who has studied your language and customs."

"Are you Israeli?" he inquires.

"No, but I've worked alongside both Arab and Jewish archaeologists in this country." I hope to ease their suspicions, to show I come in peace.

"Are you Christian?" the first man asks, his tone cautious.

"Yes," I respond, aware this could complicate things.

He shrugs, a gesture of acceptance. "You are welcome. Were you spying on our camp with those binoculars?"

I choose honesty. "I apologize for intruding, but I was concerned about your safety. There were rumors of hostile Iranians in the area, and I wanted to see if it was safe to travel here."

"They left," he replies.

"May I ask what happened?"

"They arrived yesterday morning—fifteen of them in four cars. We offered them our hospitality, as is Bedouin custom. But we were cautious; we knew they were dangerous. They left just before sunset."

"Why did they leave?" I press.

"They believed the Israeli military was coming for them."

"Did you see the Israeli military?"

"About half an hour after the Iranians left, the Israelis showed up—some from over the hill, others in four-wheel-drive vehicles."

"Where did the Iranians go?"

"They split up and took different paths. We informed the Israelis, whom we believe are Shin Bet."

"And then what happened?"

"The Shin Bet team also split up."

"Thank you for that information. I'm glad you and your families are safe."

"For now," he says, a shadow passing over his face.

"What do you mean?"

"Do you know about the war?"

"Not in detail, but I'm aware of some things."

"May we invite you for tea?" he asks, his expression softening.

"*Shukran Jazeelan*," I reply, grateful for the kindness extended to me. "I would be happy to share tea with you."

"Please, follow us," the taller man gestures.

Chapter 16

As I pull my SUV to a stop beside the Bedouin camp, I take a moment to survey the surroundings. The camp stands as a small refuge amid the vast desert expanse, anchored by two weathered trucks, one of which I recognized from my vantage point atop the hill. Three tents, their rugged structures a testament to countless desert nights, are near each other.

One of the tents stands out, its sides propped up by sturdy wooden poles, creating an inviting shaded area. Oriental rugs are strewn across the earthen floor beneath, and five camping chairs form a welcoming circle. This simple yet comfortable setup reflects the Bedouins' resourcefulness, a blend of tradition and practicality.

Caution lingers beneath my curiosity as I exit my vehicle and tread carefully toward the two men who had invited me for tea. I've encountered Bedouin camps before, drawn by the stark beauty of this region and the mysteries it conceals. Generally, these encounters have been peaceful, though the contentious relationship between Israelis and Bedouins regarding the legality of their villages occasionally casts a shadow. It's never easy to dictate to nomadic people where they can and cannot live.

Respecting their customs, I leave my shoes outside the tent before following the taller of the two men inside. The atmosphere within is warm and inviting. I'm directed to one of the camping chairs, and as I sit down, my unease slowly dissipates. The presence of two women and a little girl emerging from one of the tents suggests these men likely harbor no hostile intentions. In Bedouin culture, there exists an unwritten rule that certain behaviors are deemed unacceptable in front of women, which brings me a sense of relief.

The smaller man gives orders to the women, who immediately go to the fire pit outside to tend to the fire. Their attire is a blend of traditional and modern clothing, adorned with gold jewelry and colorful scarves covering their heads. Their thobes—long, loose cotton dresses embroidered with intricate designs—reflect a deep-seated sense of culture. I make a conscious effort not to stare, fully aware that such behavior would be considered rude.

The young girl, with curious eyes fixed on me, stands near one of the men's chairs. Her presence adds a touch of innocence to the scene, and I offer her a friendly smile, which she shyly returns.

Breaking the silence, the taller man, whom I later learn is Khalid, greets me warmly: *"Ahlan wa sahlan."* With that phrase, a wave of reassurance washes over me, and I realize I'm among friends, albeit new ones.

Soon, the women return with a pot of tea and small glasses. Khalid takes the pot from them and carefully pours the tea into our glasses. I accept it gratefully, savoring a sip as a sign of my appreciation and understanding of their customs. To refuse such an offering would be a grave offense, and I'm keen to show my respect.

In this tent, I am more than a stranger; I'm a guest, an honorary member of their family. The Bedouins' reputation for warmth and open heartedness becomes evident with every passing moment. They live by the creed, "A guest is a guest even if he is a foe," a testament to their unyielding commitment to safeguarding those they welcome under their tent, even in the face of discord.

As we sip our tea, I feel the trust they've placed in me, and I resolve to repay their kindness by respecting their customs and treading lightly in their world. The surroundings may be hostile, but the hearts of the Bedouins are anything but.

Khalid breaks the ice further, introducing himself and his brother Saleh. I respond with my name, mindful not to pry too deeply, as starting with personal questions would be impolite.

Khalid observes, "It is a warm day."

"Yes," I reply, "but I've experienced much warmer days in the Naqab." I use the Arabic name *"Al-Naqab,"* which means the barren or empty, reflecting the region's arid nature.

Their smiles indicate they appreciate my familiarity with the term. Saleh continues the conversation, asking if I know the Naqab well.

"I am an archaeologist," I explain, "and I've spent many months here on digs and exploring this land." I add, *"Al-sahra' umm al-Hayat,*" meaning the desert is the mother of life. It's a saying that conveys admiration for the barren region as a source of natural resources and the origin of many civilizations.

Once more, their smiles indicate their approval, and we share a moment of camaraderie over our tea.

I venture to ask, "Where have you been, or where do you plan to go?" This polite inquiry among nomadic Bedouins over the centuries serves as a way to exchange valuable information.

Their demeanor shifts slightly, and I wonder if I've inadvertently touched upon a sensitive topic. After a moment, Khalid responds, "We are from the town of Bir Hadaj, but we had problems there, and it wasn't safe. So, we decided to seek refuge elsewhere. Then, this war started."

Bir Hadaj is a Bedouin town about forty kilometers south of Be'er Sheva. "May I ask about the problems?" I inquire cautiously, not wanting to pry.

Saleh explains, "There's a group of thugs who came from Hebron, demanding payments. We refused, and our lives were threatened. That's when we decided to leave."

"I'm sorry to hear that," I respond sympathetically. "How long have you been here?"

"About three weeks," Khalid replies.

I'm left wondering how they've managed to survive, given the challenges of finding food, water, and gas for their trucks. I notice jerrycans in one of the vehicles, likely containing gasoline. Bedouins are known for their resourcefulness. "That's quite some time," I remark. "You mentioned the war. What are your thoughts on it?"

Saleh admits, "We fear for our brother, who is in the Israeli army. This may be the *Al-Malhama al-Kubra*, the great war, which some call Har-Magedon."

"What do you know about this war?" I ask, my academic curiosity piqued.

Khalid responds, "In *Surah Al-Anbiya*, verse 96, the Quran says that before the Day of Judgment, Gog and Magog will be released and swarm from every hill. This is one of the signs of the end times that will precede the final hour. The Quran also says in verse 97 that when this happens, the true promise of God will be near, and the eyes of the disbelievers will stare in horror."

"Yes, I've read that in your Holy Book," I acknowledge. "The Jewish Tanakh also speaks of similar events. In your understanding, who are Gog and Magog?"

As a Christian, I believe that faith in Christ alone is the only way to enter a relationship with God. Still, out of academic curiosity I've read the holy books of many religions. My grandfather said that it is important to know the worldview of others to better understand them and speak to them.

Khalid explains, "Some of our scholars say they are allegorical figures, while others believe they are real people, descendants of Japheth, one of the sons of Noah, who settled in the regions of Asia and Europe after the great flood. Some even speculate that they could represent empires like Russia or China, but the truth remains unclear. All we know is that many armies now surround Israel."

I share their concern about the war, the very reason I sought refuge away from Jerusalem. "Only our Father in Heaven knows," I say, "but we see the signs. Are you planning to stay here?" I purposely use the word Father because in Islam there is no concept of God as 'Father' in a personal or familial sense. This differentiates our beliefs.

Khalid nods in understanding. He replies, "We must move on. There is little water."

In Bedouin culture, valuable information is exchanged among nomads, so I decide to share some insights: "To the east of here, near Eilat, there are caves with springs. That might be a safer place to go."

"So, we've heard," Khalid acknowledges.

"That's where I'm headed," I say. "Perhaps we'll meet there."

"It would be our pleasure," Khalid responds warmly.

Before I depart, one last question lingers in my mind. "During the Israeli army's operation, when they split up and followed the Iranians, did you happen to see a tall Israeli woman with dark hair and blue eyes?"

"Yes," Khalid confirms. "She seemed to be a leader."

"Can you recall which direction she went?"

Saleh, the younger brother, offers an answer, "She was in a vehicle heading east."

"Thank you for your hospitality and assistance," I say, grateful for their openness.

I rise from my seat, offering handshakes and heartfelt gratitude before returning to my car. In the back, I find a bag of dates and dried figs, a gift given to Ariela and me by the mayor of Mitzpe Ramon. I place a kilo of the sweet treats in an unused plastic bag.

With the bag in hand, I return to Khalid and say, "I wish you all the best and hope we may meet again someday. May our Father in Heaven bless and protect you and your family."

He takes the bag, peers inside, and utters a heartfelt "*Shukran.*"

As I get back into my car and head east, my heart is heavy with thoughts of Ariela and the uncertain future of the Bedouin family.

Chapter 17

The Negev sprawls out before me, a vast, arid expanse that makes up a significant portion of Israel's landscape but is home to only a fraction of its population. Most people cluster in the bustling cities of Be'er Sheva and Eilat, leaving the rest to reside in scattered small towns like Mitzpe Ramon or agricultural settlements. Others choose isolation, retreating from the modern world for reasons known only to them. Hermits have called this rugged terrain home for centuries, while Khalid and his family now find themselves forced into a nomadic existence, embracing the traditions of their ancestors.

Driving away from the Bedouin camp feels like stepping out of a time machine, moving from the warmth of their ancient customs. I can't help contrasting that with Tel Aviv—a city pulsing with high-tech innovations, skyscrapers, and vibrant life. How is it doing in these tumultuous times?

I find myself alone again, the desert stretching out in every direction. Cautiously, I navigate the winding road, not only to protect my vehicle but also because I am uncertain of what lies ahead. This route leads east to both my cave in Eilat and the path Ariela might have taken. The urgency of either destination weighs on me, but I can't determine which pulls at me more.

Khalid and Saleh's conversation about verses from the Quran lingers in my mind, echoing alongside references from Ezekiel and Daniel. I wonder if the Prophet Muhammad used these sources in his revelations. It's a stark reminder that the signs of the end times aren't confined to Christian and Jewish narratives; the Islamic tradition, too, anticipates these apocalyptic events.

With the car radio offering only crackles, I am left in darkness regarding the war's progress. Will Western nations intervene as they have for years, or will they remain passive observers as this conflict escalates? Doubts linger, casting shadows over my thoughts.

The Book of Daniel speaks of a cunning, ruthless world leader, a notion echoed in the Book of Revelation. I'm unsure of who that might be, but I have my theories. This ties into something referred to as the revived Roman Empire. What exactly does that entail?

Some argue it pertains to Europe, while others claim it includes all nations influenced by the Roman Empire—Europe, the United States, and beyond.

Once again, I am confronted with my ignorance regarding the complexities of end-times prophecies. While I have explored historical sites tied to the New Testament—Capernaum, Jerusalem, and the Pool of Siloam—my knowledge of the future remains painfully limited.

As I drive, a fork in the road emerges, prompting me to stop and assess the tire tracks left behind. Khalid and Saleh mentioned that the four vehicles belonging to the Quds Force and Shin Bet teams had split up, heading in different directions. Now, I see fresh tire tracks—two vehicles have taken the eastern route, while two others veered northward.

What is happening here? The Quds Force operatives are not amateurs; they combine lethal combat skills with modern warfare tactics. Their expertise spans bomb-making, drone operation, and satellite awareness, along with intimate knowledge of Israel's surveillance capabilities. With most of Israel's resources focused on tracking larger armies to the north and south, the operatives' decision to split into four cars and disperse is a calculated maneuver, making drone surveillance difficult.

I worry about Ariela, yet I can't ignore the foolishness of pursuing her into a battlefield. Why drive headlong into a conflict involving highly trained Quds Force soldiers? My rational mind urges me to continue to my destination near Eilat, but my emotions refuse to be silenced.

An hour passes, and the sun beats down mercilessly. My stomach growls, forcing me to stop. I pull into a wadi, seeking refuge from the heat. Emerging from the car, I find a shaded spot and unpack a simple meal—a piece of pita bread, a small can of hummus, and a bottle of water.

As I split the pita and generously spread the hummus, I savor each bite, appreciating the nourishing blend of protein, fiber, and healthy fats. It provides a moment of solace, a brief respite from the journey ahead.

After I finish, fatigue washes over me. I stretch out on the sandy ground beneath the shade of a large rock, letting my eyes drift shut as the tranquility envelops me. For a moment, I forget the chaos of the outside world.

Then, as if from a distant realm, the dissonance of gunfire breaks the silence. Rapid shots echo in the distance, one after another, followed by an eerie hush. Am I dreaming, lost in exhaustion, or is this a reality I cannot ignore?

Fear creeps in. Should I hide? Or flee in the opposite direction? The shots seem to originate from the east, but the mountainous acoustics play tricks on the mind, bouncing sounds in unpredictable ways.

I return to my car, grab my rifle, and secure my handgun in its holster. Ten minutes pass, and the silence remains unbroken. Tentatively, I restart the engine, pull back onto the dirt road, and cautiously inch my way eastward.

Chapter 18

I navigate the dirt road, and my foot is easy on the accelerator. I am driving into the unknown, toward a destination that could hold unimaginable danger. A simple archaeologist like me is ill-equipped for this kind of peril.

What lies ahead on this lonely road? Are commandos from both sides—Israelis and Iranians—locked in a deadly confrontation, their bullets tearing through the air with ruthless precision? Is Ariela caught in the crossfire, her fate in danger of fragile hope?

My mind races, struggling to comprehend the reality behind the rapid gunfire that shattered the stillness. This is no single shot fired by a lone hunter; it's calculated and persistent—the unmistakable noise of a firefight.

The stark truth grips me: I cannot possibly confront a team of trained military operatives, especially those as formidable as the Quds Force. My only advantage lies in discretion, in avoiding confrontation rather than seeking it out. What could I do against them? My handgun feels like a feeble weapon in the face of such danger.

I glance nervously from the rearview mirror to rocky hills in front of me, scanning for any signs of movement. Every twist and turn of the road become a potential ambush, every rocky outcrop a possible hiding place.

The logical part of my mind urges me to retreat, to turn back and find safety, to abandon the curiosity that has led me down this treacherous path. But my stubborn heart echoes with the haunting question of Ariela's fate.

In this moment, I silently vow not to foolishly rush into the abyss of danger.

As the road enters a narrow gorge flanked by high cliffs casting shadows over the uneven terrain, my instincts scream that this is the perfect place for an ambush.

Then, up ahead, I see something familiar—a car, unmistakably one driven by the Israeli Shin Bet team. Relief and dread intertwine as I stop my vehicle and grab my binoculars to survey the scene. There's no movement, no sign of life. Could this be the car Ariela was in? Anticipation weighs heavily as I prepare myself for what I might discover.

I turn off the engine and step out, holding my rifle in a ready position while my handgun remains holstered. Each footstep is measured and deliberate as I move from one hiding spot to another, my breath shallow with anxiety.

When I reach the car, I am met with a nightmare. Three members of the Israeli Shin Bet team lie sprawled on the ground, their clothes stained with the evidence of violence. Dread constricts my throat as I check each man, fingers trembling as I search for a faint pulse. The first two offer no solace; their stillness confirms their fate.

But with the third, there's a glimmer of hope. I find a pulse—feeble but persistent—a fragile thread of life amidst death's grip. His eyes flutter open as I touch his neck, a glazed gaze of pain and confusion meeting mine.

"We were ambushed," he rasps, blood trickling from a wound on his head. The gravity of his words sends a shiver down my spine, and I am overwhelmed by the urgency of the situation.

My mind races. There's a first aid kit in my car, but will it be enough to save this man's life? Desperation gnaws at my thoughts, yet I cannot allow panic to cloud my judgment.

"Where are the others?" he asks, concern lacing his voice as he glances toward his fallen colleagues, resignation in his eyes.

"There are two men over there, your colleagues, but I'm sorry to say they didn't make it."

"And Esti?" he inquires, his voice wavering.

"A woman?" I ask, desperate to understand.

"Yes, Esti."

"There's no woman here," I reply, dread curling in my stomach.

"They must have her," he murmurs, his voice fading.

"I'm sorry," I say, at a loss. Then, thinking of Ariela, I ask, "What direction did Ariela go?"

"Ariela?" Confusion clouds his eyes. "Yes, Ariela, the woman I brought to the meeting point yesterday. Tall, dark hair, blue eyes?"

"Oh, yes," he murmurs, pain distorting his words. "She goes by Ariela on missions, but her name is Esti Yitzhak. The Iranians must have her. This is terrible."

My mind races to grasp the significance of his revelation. "What do you mean?" I urge him.

"Esti is the daughter of the Prime Minister. Now she's in the hands of the enemy. You must find her. Get help." His voice drops to a whisper, and I feel time slipping through my fingers.

Helpless in the face of his deteriorating condition, I watch as his breaths grow shallow and strained, his life fading like sand through an hourglass. I want to rush back to my car for water or first aid supplies, but a grim realization dawns: it's too late.

His voice falls silent, his final breath escaping into the air.

Chapter 19

There are moments in life when helplessness wraps around you like a vice, and I find myself firmly ensnared. Witnessing a corpse is one thing, but watching a life slip away—powerless to intervene—is a torment of its own kind.

Before me lies the grim sight of three men who were alive and well just a day ago. The man who just died spoke of an ambush and mentioned Ariela's abduction, or rather, Esti Yitzhak, as I now know her real name. Questions swarm in my mind. Did the ambushers realize her true identity? Were they from the Quds Force or some other faction? Most urgently, where have they taken Ariela? Their path must lead eastward, for they didn't cross my route on the way here.

Contemplating what to do with these dead men weighs heavily on me. I wonder about their communication capabilities and whether anyone at their headquarters knows of their current predicament. Leaving them here isn't an option. One by one, I move them into their vehicle. I may not have the build of a weightlifter, but I'm tall and strong—years spent toiling on archaeological digs have given me sinewy muscles. The physical task is manageable; it's the psychological toll that grips me.

Once the three men are inside their vehicle, I gather their rifles, handguns, ammunition, clips, and flashbangs, adding to my growing arsenal. I'm not entirely sure why I keep accumulating these weapons instead of discarding them. It was Ariela who collected arms, and I find myself unconsciously following her example.

Thinking of her, I make my way to the Israelis' vehicle to retrieve her travel bag. It feels like a futile act, but if someone finds her, she will need her things. After securing the weapons and Ariela's bag in my car, I survey the scene, inspecting both sides of the road.

The ground reveals knee and toe prints, indicating someone knelt, while larger shoe prints stand nearby. I can easily envision Ariela in that moment—cautious yet defiant. A few paces away, the earth tells a more disturbing story; it shows signs of her being dragged. I know her footprint well.

Following the prints leads me to tire tracks—evidence of a hidden car positioned behind a massive rock. Beyond her footprints, blood droplets stain the ground. Is it her or one of her assailants being wounded? Is it a mortal injury?

That's all the information I can glean from this site. Now, I must act. The Israeli Shin Bet agent urged me to seek help, and he's likely right, but where can I go? I'm a considerable distance from Mitzpe Ramon. The nearest option appears to be the road running parallel to the border fence, where Israeli troops are stationed, according to Ariela's accounts and the young Israeli soldiers, Oded and Naomi.

Consulting my GPS, I estimate it to be about fifteen kilometers away, reachable in thirty to sixty minutes if I can find a road leading in that direction.

I start my car's engine and head east, my gaze scanning for a road branching southward toward the border fence. Adrenaline radiates through me, driven by a desperate need to act.

Another reckless notion flits through my mind. What if, instead of seeking help, I track down Ariela and her captors? It's a foolhardy idea, a David-versus-Goliath fantasy. Still, the mere thought of Ariela's perilous situation pushes me to consider it. But what could I possibly do against them? The question reverberates in my mind like a persistent echo.

Pushing the vehicle to its limits, my tires weave around potholes, accelerating whenever the road permits.

My thoughts churn with a shocking revelation: Ariela is Esti Yitzhak, the daughter of the current Prime Minister of Israel. There are no accusations of dishonesty against her; I understand the methods of Shin Bet. When on a mission, they often assume alternate identities. But a mystery remains—why would the daughter of someone in such a crucial position willingly place herself in harm's way? Her capture could provide leverage to her father's enemies.

I reflect on the events of the past months, where the Israeli government has been mired in conflict—a sad reality all too common in this country. The political parties in Israel had become increasingly fragmented, with threats being made. There were even misguided speculations of civil war as opposing factions grew increasingly entrenched. Finally, a fragile compromise was reached, and Zevi Yitzhak recently assumed the role of Prime Minister. However, his government remains precarious, with cabinet members holding opposing positions. I'm sure this instability factors into the calculations of the countries amassing on Israel's borders, seizing the opportunity to strike while the nation is at its weakest.

The burning question in my mind revolves around Ariela's involvement with Shin Bet. Kahlid and Saleh, back at the Bedouin camp, regarded her as a leader, suggesting she has been with Shin Bet for some time—likely enlisting just after completing her mandatory service in the Israeli Defense Forces. If I guess her age correctly, she could have served in Shin Bet for seven years or more.

Once her father ascended to the role of Prime Minister, a dilemma must have arisen. Shin Bet operates under the direct authority of the Prime Minister. With her father in office, does he pull her from Shin Bet to ensure her safety, or does she continue to serve? Politics in Israel can be brutal, and opposition politicians would undoubtedly exploit any decision he made. If he withdrew her from Shin Bet, they'd accuse him of nepotism, claiming he used his position to shield his child from danger. Given the multitude of challenges he faces, I imagine he deferred the decision, creating an agonizing predicament. And knowing Ariela, I'm convinced she insisted on staying with Shin Bet.

Now, Zevi Yitzhak, the Israeli Prime Minister, finds himself in an unenviable position. Those holding his daughter would demand an astronomical ransom—not just in monetary terms, but in the political damage it would generate. With so much already on his plate, such a distraction is the last thing he needs.

Freeing Esti Yitzhak from her captors is paramount, not only for her sake but for the sake of the entire nation of Israel.

Chapter 20

The last words of the Israeli operative echo relentlessly in my mind, a cryptic puzzle begging for resolution. "You must find her. Get help." The contradiction in his plea gnaws at me. Should I confront unknown dangers alone in my pursuit of her, or should I seek assistance? The urgency of her plight propels me forward, intensifying my resolve.

A chilling unease settles in my gut as I ponder Ariela's plight. Is she imprisoned in the backseat of her captives' car, or is she subjected to the horrors concealed within the trunk? Reason tells me that the trunk likely contains the captor's gear, leaving the backseat as the probable location for her. Yet, the grim knowledge of the Iranian military's brutal methods leads my imagination down darker paths, especially what they might do to a woman.

I slam on the brakes before reaching a fork in the road, dust swirling in my wake. Leaping from the car, I scrutinize the tire tracks imprinted in the dirt before me. They tell a story as old as time—the last vehicle to travel this way took the eastern route, steering clear of the southern path that leads to the border fence.

The choice ahead is stark and unyielding. A singular purpose drives me: Ariela's safety. The relentless ticking of time offers no solace. I picture Ariela, confined and in danger, propelling me toward a quick decision.

I inhale deeply, the dry air filling my lungs, and commit to my path. There will be no wasting time veering south. I accelerate along the eastern road, my foot heavy on the gas pedal.

As the road winds through a gorge, I ease off the accelerator. Emerging from the twists and turns, a long, straight stretch unfurls ahead, reaching over a mile into the horizon. A glint in the distance catches my eye—a flash of light that could be a beacon, possibly a car pulling off the road.

I swiftly grab my binoculars, squinting at the distant vehicle. The sun's glare dances on its surface, obscuring any view of who might be inside. It vanishes into a gully, its destination shrouded from my sight.

A plan begins to form. I guide my car forward a few hundred yards and find a hiding spot behind a rocky outcrop. I gather essential supplies into my backpack—water, a couple of energy bars, four additional clips for my weapons, and my binoculars. I shoulder my rifle, ensure my handgun is secure in my holster, and secure my hunting knife. With determination, I set out on foot.

The distance is rough—perhaps half a mile. The rugged landscape demands caution, compelling me to navigate from one vantage point to another, with every movement calculated and eyes peeled for threats.

After an exhausting hour and a half of trekking, I finally reach the summit of a hill overlooking the gully where the car disappeared. I slide forward, trembling hands gripping my binoculars, bridging the gap between me and the scene below.

There it is—the car, trunk wide open, and two men busily arranging a makeshift camp nearby.

On the barren ground, Ariela sits, her wrists bound by plastic ties. She watches her captors with an unwavering gaze. I can hear their voices drifting on the dry wind, speaking in Arabic, some words just within earshot.

These men are not Quds Force; their language betrays them. Arabic and Iranian are distinct, each with unique origins and grammatical structures. Ariela had mentioned suspected collaborators in the Negev working with Iranian operatives.

A stream of fear courses through me. Freeing Ariela is my priority, but I am just one man against this formidable threat. I consider my options. Could I eliminate both men from this height? It seems unlikely; my aim is far from reliable.

With two hours of daylight left and the encroaching shadow of night, I know I must wait. First, I scan for possible routes down to the camp, selecting the best access point. Much depends on how the captors treat Ariela. They seem relaxed, perhaps waiting for someone.

Minutes stretch into an agonizing hour. The sun dips lower, casting long shadows across the hills, and the moment is drawing near.

Ariela's eyes dart around like a cat's, keenly observing every detail, contrasting sharply with the two men, engrossed in their conversation. Suddenly, her gaze lifts, and through my binoculars,

I catch her nodding slightly, looking away to mask my presence. She knows I'm out here—not a guardian angel, but a potential ally.

As stars begin to pierce the darkening sky, I make my decision. The cloak of night will be my ally. Once my eyes adjust to the dim light, I descend the rugged hillside, every step calculated to avoid dislodging even a pebble. The night holds its breath as I move like a shadow, silent and unseen.

The dry wash becomes my pathway as I inch closer to the camp. They gather around a small fire, their loud voices and laughter a facade of security. Their conversation drifts toward the destruction of Israel and the rise of a caliphate.

Now within range, I can make out their faces, illuminated by the flickering glow of the fire. They are oblivious to the danger lurking nearby. Ariela remains firmly in my line of sight, a constant reminder of the stakes.

I push forward, adrenaline surging through my veins. The time for hesitation has passed. Drawing a final breath, I step into the warm light of the campfire. Everything sharpens, narrowing down to a singular goal as I raise my rifle, the metallic click of the safety disengaging.

The captors' faces twist in shock as I disrupt their false sense of security. "Raise your hands!" I command in Arabic, my voice cutting through the night like a whip.

In a flurry of panic, one reaches for his firearm, and I fire my rifle, the shot missing him but serving as a warning. Both men raise their hands.

"Keep them up, and don't move!" I shout, my finger trembling on the trigger.

They comply.

Ariela, still bound, cautiously watches. She understands this isn't over; a novice wields the gun, steering the course of events.

With their weapons now out of reach, the captors are at my mercy. Yet their desperation renders them unpredictable, and I tread carefully, my rifle trained on them. I regret not setting my weapon to automatic fire, but fiddling with the lever now would be too risky.

"Who are you?" one stammers, his voice angry.

"That's not important," I reply, my tone firm. "What matters is the young woman you've kidnapped. Stand up, step back five paces, and you may walk away from this."

Their exchanged glances reveal a tumult of emotions. They know they are cornered, their options dwindling, and the power balance has shifted.

With a final shared look, they rise and walk backward five paces, hands still in the air.

"Now sit down," I command.

They obey, distancing themselves from their weapons. With my rifle aimed at them in one hand, I reach for my hunting knife with the other, cutting the zip tie around Ariela's wrists before handing her the knife. She quickly frees herself from the ties binding her ankles and rises, her legs shaky but determined. I tap my holster with my free hand, and Ariela nods slightly, accepting my handgun.

A sense of relief washes over me—she's far more adept with firearms than I am.

Suddenly, one of the men lunges for his weapon. Instinct takes over, and Ariela and I fire simultaneously. He collapses, lifeless, before my feet.

But the danger is far from over. The second man, undeterred by his comrade's fate, charges toward me. Ariela fires, striking him as well, but the momentum carries his body crashing into me. I tumble backward, the impact reminiscent of my high school football days.

Fueled by adrenaline, I manage to kick the assailant off me, and he thuds to the ground, unmoving. I scramble to my feet, my body trembling from the confrontation. Gasping for breath, I steady myself, hands resting on my knees, taking deep gulps of air before standing tall again. I retrieve my rifle, which had slipped from my grasp.

Ariela, her handgun still aimed at the fallen men, breaks the silence. "You speak Arabic, after all," she remarks with a wry smile, a flicker of humor.

I nod, a sense of camaraderie blooming between us despite our grim circumstances. "Not as well as Hebrew, but almost."

Her gaze softens with gratitude. "Thank you for coming. You're the last person I expected to see."

I offer a faint smile in return. "It's a strange twist of fate, but I'm here."

Her expression shifts to seriousness. "We need to leave—now."

"Why?" I ask, seeing the urgency in her tone.

Her eyes flicker toward the shadows creeping along the horizon. "Quds Force is on its way here. These two had set up a meeting to hand me over to them."

Chapter 21

Ariela moves with the precision of a seasoned operative, gathering weapons and wallets from the fallen men. She carefully stows everything in the back seat of their car, her movements fluid and efficient. "Where's your car?" she asks, her voice steady.

"About a kilometer down the road," I reply.

"Let's go," she says, slipping into the driver's seat.

I take my place in the passenger side, relieved to find the keys in the ignition. As the engine roars to life, she flicks on the headlights, and I guide her back along the winding road to where my car is parked.

We disembark, and Ariela conducts a meticulous search of their car. Moments later, she emerges holding a satellite phone. "This is how they communicated with the Quds Force and other insurgents," she explains.

"Who were they?" I inquire, anxiety creeping into my voice.

Ariela's gaze hardens. "Locals. Not everyone here is an ally. External terrorists have trained some. Those men supported the Quds Force."

"Are there more of them?"

"Our intelligence suggests there are," she replies.

"Do we know who the other hostile locals are?"

"Not yet, but identifying where these men came from could lead us to them."

She pulls out their wallets, sorting through papers before holding up their identity cards. "I need to relay this information to my headquarters. It could help find other hostiles operating in this region. Can you open the back of your car?"

I do as she asks, and Ariela deftly loads the two men's weapons into the trunk, filling nearly every available inch.

"We need to get out of here," I insist.

"Just a moment. Do you have any matches?"

I retrieve a box from the glove compartment and hand it to her. She instructs, "Start your car and move it away from here. Wait for me."

As I roll my car to a safer distance, I catch Ariela's actions in the rearview mirror. She performs a mysterious task at the back of the men's vehicle, igniting a match before sprinting toward mine and sliding inside. "Go."

I slam my foot on the accelerator, and in an instant, flames engulf the men's car. A fireball erupts, lighting up the night sky as we drive past the turnoff, where the two bodies lie near a smoldering campfire. I steer eastward, the headlights slicing through the blackness.

With one hand on the wheel, I reach behind me and grab a bottle of water, passing it to Ariela. I also pull out an energy bar from my backpack and offer it to her.

"Thank you," she murmurs, her eyes reflecting gratitude. "You seem to anticipate my needs."

"I figured you didn't eat or drink much today."

"You're right," she admits, her voice softening. "My colleagues back there at the ambush—did any of them survive?"

Breaking that kind of news is never easy. She's Israeli, and I prefer to be direct. "Unfortunately, none of them made it. They were your friends, and I can't imagine the pain you're going through, especially after what you endured."

"Everything feels like a nightmare," she replies, her voice quivering. "We like to think we're trained to handle these situations, but it's an illusion. It feels like someone has ripped my soul out."

"I'm sorry," I offer sincerely.

Ariela falls silent, and I respect her need for solitude. I have my own demons to confront, grappling with the aftershocks of killing a man and then being crashed into by another. What began as a desperate escape to the desert has morphed into something more profound. Perhaps my journey wasn't purely about selfish escapism. Maybe there's a greater purpose at play.

For what feels like an eternity, Ariela remains lost in thought. Although I'm curious about her reflections, I allow her the silence she requires. Finally, she retrieves the satellite phone she had placed on the floorboard and fiddles with the buttons. A light blinks on.

"We're well past the campsite of those two terrorists," she says, her tone resolute. "I want to try to contact my headquarters. Can you pull over?"

I steer the car off the road, unsure of why I'm doing this. There's no one else around. After turning off the headlights, I shut off the engine.

"Do you have a flashlight?" she asks.

"In the glove compartment."

She reaches into the compartment, taking my flashlight along with the men's wallets and the satellite phone before getting out of the car. I watch as she walks away, her silhouette fading into the darkness.

Dialing a number, she launches into a rapid conversation, her voice emphatic. illuminating the identity cards with the flashlight. She turns off the light, pockets the cards, and continues her discussion. It sounds like she's giving an update, but then it escalates into a heated argument. I see her hand extend as if she's emphasizing a crucial point.

When she returns to the car, she climbs in and says, "We can go?"

I start the engine, switch on the headlights, and ask, "Go where?"

"Someplace safe. I've been ordered to disengage from this mission and find refuge until further notice or until this war is settled."

Chapter 22

The clock on my dashboard flashes 1:00 a.m. The journey is slow, hampered by the darkness and a road riddled with treacherous bumps.

Fatigue weighs heavily on me. My day began at dawn, nerves frayed and on high alert, with only a brief respite at the Bedouin camp.

Ariela sits beside me, valiantly trying to remain alert, but fatigue often claims her, luring her into brief bouts of sleep.

"We should find a place to rest for the night," I suggest, mindful of our need for sleep.

"I agree," she replies, her voice heavy with the day's burdens.

"In the morning, we can discuss your destination," She may want to go to Eilat, although I already have a location in mind for myself—a remote cave with a natural spring.

As is my habit, I search for a secluded spot off the road, a quiet refuge from prying eyes. I bring the car to a stop, and from the back, I retrieve Ariela's travel bag and hand it to her. Surprise is in her eyes.

Forgoing our usual camp rituals, we roll out our ground pads and lay down our sleeping bags. Wordlessly, we undress and slip into our bags. Ariela's presence nearby brings me a measure of comfort. I resist the urge to dwell on the grim events of the day, choosing instead to close my eyes and embrace the solace of sleep.

In the early morning light, I awaken to the sight of Ariela beside me, my surroundings coming into focus. Our eyes meet, and a smile graces her lips.

"*Boker tov*," she greets.

"*Boker tov*," I reply, stretching. "Have you been awake long?"

"No, surprisingly, I slept quite well."

We both rise, dressing pragmatically as we prepare for the day. Yet, my gaze can't help but linger on the contours of her lithe form, stirring emotions beneath the surface.

I retrieve the camping stove and brew coffee as we share another breakfast of oatmeal garnished with chopped dates and figs. The routine feels almost comforting, yet the truth of our situation remains inescapable.

Once breakfast is finished and everything is packed away, I ask, "What orders did you receive last night?"

"I was instructed to find a secure location."

"Given the current circumstances, how does your organization define 'secure'?" I hesitate to mention 'Shin Bet'; it's likely not something she'd openly admit.

She nods. "A senior-level person gave the order, and he meant to go secretly in a place where I am unlikely to be discovered. And of course to stay away from any Quds Force enemies or any other terrorists."

"Okay, so where do you need to go?"

"I'm not sure yet. What about you?"

"I'm heading to a cave not far from Eilat. It's in a remote location, hard to find, and it has a reliable water source."

"Can I come with you?"

"Ariela, you're more than welcome."

Those words echo in my mind, reminding me to regain my focus. Traveling with Esti Yitzhak, the Prime Minister's daughter—albeit under an alias—carries its risks. Someone might recognize her. I understand why she was ordered to find safety; the consequences of her capture would be severe. There's too much at stake for them to be sidetracked by such considerations. It would be wiser for her to go into hiding.

It strikes me as strange that her superiors didn't instruct her to return to their headquarters in Tel Aviv or Jerusalem. They must have acted swiftly, and Israelis are known for their tactical acumen.

Still, I can't deny the comfort Ariela's company brings. Our shared experiences have forged a bond. Plus, there's another practical reason for her to stay with me: she's a trained military operative, well-versed in weapons. And then there's the unsettling thought of a car full of firearms. Of all people, she'd know how to handle them.

We return to the car, knowing the Quds Force operatives are out there. We drive on.

Chapter 23

We are about twenty kilometers from my hidden cave, traversing a well-worn dirt road defined by centuries of travelers crossing over this taxing wasteland. The arid expanse of the Negev stretches around us, a landscape that conceals both peril and life-sustaining secrets.

One such secret—a year-round spring—lies just off the road. Its clear waters feed a small pond no larger than a bathtub. For generations, this spot has served as a lifeline for weary travelers and a source of water for wild animals.

Finding water in the Negev is no small feat, but it is possible. Well-known locations like Ein Gedi, perched on the western shore of the Dead Sea, are celebrated for their freshwater springs and pools. David himself sought refuge there while fleeing Saul, a place that echoes biblical tales of survival and cunning.

Other springs, such as Ein Avdat, once home to Nabateans and Catholic monks, boast waterfalls and stunning canyons. Ein Avdat flows year-round and is protected within the Ein Avdat Nature Reserve. These details would undoubtedly intrigue any archaeologist hoping to unravel the secrets of this arid land.

With purpose, I pull the car over to the side of the road, where Tamarisk shrubs and Acacia trees flourish alongside four date palms, their roots digging deep into the dry earth. A traveler from long ago must have dropped date seeds here, and the moisture allowed them to flourish.

Stepping out of the car, I grab two cups and say to Ariela, "Let's have a drink."

She joins me, curiosity shining in her eyes as she surveys the area. "What is this place?"

"A little oasis—emphasis on 'little,'" I reply with a wry smile. "There's a freshwater source hidden among those shrubs."

We lock the car and wander through the greenery until we reach a shaded cliff where water trickles from the rocks. It takes just moments to fill a cup, which I hand to Ariela.

She takes a sip, her expression brightening as the coolness refreshes her. "This is incredibly refreshing."

I fill my cup, reflecting on the paradox of this land with its scorching days and frigid nights, where shaded rocks preserve the chill of the water.

As we drink, the serenity of the moment provides a brief reprieve from the horrors of our night and the chaos of the day that preceded it.

Suddenly, a noise in the brush disrupts the peace. Two men emerge, one of them brandishing a rifle and leveling it at me. "Give car keys," he demands in broken Hebrew, his intentions unmistakable: neutralize me and steal the car.

But Ariela is quicker than he anticipates, drawing her pistol and aiming it at him. "Drop it," she commands.

Caught in a no-win situation, the man hesitates. Shooting me would provoke her retaliation, and turning the gun on Ariela would yield the same fate. His companion realizes their precarious position and signals to lower the weapon. Defeated, the armed man drops his gun to the ground. Seizing the opportunity, I pull my handgun from my holster, and now they find themselves with two guns trained on them. Cautiously, I walk to the man, bend down, and take his rifle, hoping he does not make the same impulsive mistake as the two men who held Ariela captive.

Relieved that I am no longer in the crosshairs, I ask the obvious question. "What do you want?"

Ariela states the blunt truth. "They're robbers."

The men remain silent.

Unyielding, Ariela extends her arm menacingly, aiming her weapon at the man's head. "Where are you from?"

"Hebron."

"That's a long way. How did you get here?" I ask.

"By truck," he replies.

"Then take us to it," I demand.

The two men lead us along a narrow path, and soon, we discover a pickup truck hidden behind the bushes. The truck's bed is filled with boxes overflowing with food and clothing.

"Did you steal this from travelers?" I inquire.

"It's ours," one of them insists.

I pry open one of the boxes and find women's clothing inside. A wave of anger surges through me as I envision the unfortunate woman from whom these items were taken. Did these robbers abandon their victims in this harsh desert, leaving them to fend for themselves?

I see the same emotions reflected in Ariela's eyes. "Both of you are going to walk home," she declares sternly.

The men's faces twist in fear. "It's over two hundred kilometers to Hebron," one protests.

"Perhaps you'll make it. Perhaps not," I reply cryptically.

Inside their truck's cab, I spot two bottles of water resting on the floor, likely filled from this very spring. I hand the bottles to the men. "This should help. You might make it. Now, go."

With the water bottles clutched tightly, they retreat, following a trail that disappears into the rolling hills. Once they're out of sight, Ariela and I are left alone with our thoughts.

"They deserve prison," Ariela states, her voice firm.

I can't help but nod in agreement. "Absolutely. But for now, there's not much we can do except leave them to the wasteland's brand of justice. What about all this?" I gesture toward the stolen goods in the truck.

"The thought of keeping stolen property doesn't sit right with me," Ariela admits. "My heart aches for those who lost it. If we're lucky, we can return some of it to the rightful owners. But letting it go to waste here isn't an option."

With a shared understanding, we head back to the spring for more water. Just as we settle in, another rustle in the brush makes us both instinctively draw our handguns, aiming them at the source of the noise.

Chapter 24

For a solitary man who spends his days sifting through sand and examining ancient artifacts, the last two days have been an unbearable trial. My nerves are frayed from the bombs, the confrontations with terrorists and robbers, and all the close calls with danger. The noise in the brush is like the straw that broke the camel's back; I'm not ready to face more ordeals. Both Ariela and I have our weapons drawn, ready for whatever emerges from the underbrush.

Then, from the dense foliage, a familiar figure appears—one I recognize instantly. It's Brother Taizé, a solitary hermit who calls these bleak lands home.

"Hello, Thomas," he greets me with a warm smile and gentle voice as if we were old friends meeting after only a day apart. I remember the last time I gave him a ride to Eilat, a brief encounter that lingers in my memory.

Brother Taizé is a man of mystery and wisdom. Now, he moves with deliberate purpose as he pushes a rickety, rusty wheelbarrow laden with two large plastic jerry cans. His silver hair, bleached by the relentless sun, tumbles down to his shoulders in a wild tangle. A trimmed beard gives his weathered face—a deep, leathery brown from years spent in the sun—a distinguished look. His deep-set eyes, the color of faded denim, seem to harbor timeless wisdom, and the crinkles around them tell stories of countless days in quiet contemplation.

Despite his lean, sinewy frame, he radiates an indefinable strength, as though the very desert has molded him into a monument of resilience. He wears a simple, faded beige robe that flutters softly in the breeze, its fabric threadbare from years of wear and travel. His well-worn sandals protect his calloused feet from the harsh terrain.

As he approaches, a calmness envelops us, and I gesture for Ariela to lower her weapon.

"Hello, Brother Taizé," I say, feeling my heart rate settle at the sight of him.

"How are you?" he asks, his concern genuine.

"It's a hectic time," I reply, glancing at Ariela. "And you?"

"Life has its rhythms, but I understand the increase in activity," he replies, eyes thoughtful.

"What do you mean?" I ask, intrigued.

"For the past few days, the road has been busy. More people stop here for water, making their way toward Eilat. I just saw two men walking northeast."

"They are robbers who were persuaded to go home," I state, a grimness lacing my tone.

"Ah, 'Thou shalt not steal' is a strong command," he remarks, a hint of sorrow in his voice.

Ariela shifts her weight, keenly listening to our conversation, and I make the introductions. "Brother Taizé, this is my friend Ariela. And Ariela, please meet Brother Taizé."

"It is my pleasure," he says warmly.

Never one to shy away from asking questions, Ariela dives in. "How do you know each other?"

"Whenever I find myself in this corner of the world," I begin, "Brother Taizé seems to cross my path."

He chuckles softly as he approaches the spring, setting one of his jerry cans to capture the precious water trickling from the rocks. I seize this moment to provide Ariela with insight into my enigmatic acquaintance. "He's a hermit, an ascetic, reminiscent of the desert fathers from early Christianity. He spent his youth at Taizé, a monastery retreat in France, before choosing this life of meditation in the desert. No one knows his real name or where he hails from; he's known only as Brother Taizé."

Ariela's curiosity simmers. "Where does he live?"

"Nearby, but I've never been there," I reply.

As the jerry can fills, Brother Taizé returns to us, curiosity etched on his weathered face. "What brings you to this place?"

"Have you heard about what's happening, the war?" I ask, sensing the heaviness in the air.

"Indeed. It's a prophecy long foretold," he responds, his gaze piercing yet serene.

"What do you mean?" Ariela interjects, her interest piqued.

"This," Brother Taizé begins, "is vividly described in the Book of Revelation. We stand at the threshold of a new era, one where the Messiah is poised to enter."

Ariela, eyes narrowing skeptically, asks, "What do you know?"

"Please sit," he gestures toward the shaded area beneath the palm trees. "This is not a quick topic."

As we settle down, anticipation hangs in the air. "The desert has always held a sacred significance in the spiritual realm," Brother Taizé continues, his voice rich with conviction. "It's a place of revelation and transformation. The Children of Israel spent forty years here, learning about God's ways. Just as the prophets of old sought solitude to commune with the divine, we find ourselves once more amidst prophecies and revelations."

His eyes drift toward the hill behind the spring. "Where to begin? Ezekiel spoke of the vision of dry bones, a symbol of resurrection and hope for the Jews. Even in turmoil, there is potential for rebirth and renewal."

Ariela leans forward, frustration evident, wanting a straightforward answer. "And what of your Book of Revelation? What does it say?"

"We will get there, but let me begin with the Book of Daniel," he replies, a faint smile illuminating his features. "Within Daniel's visions lie understandings of kingdoms rising and falling, of powerful empires that will meet their fate in the hands of a higher power—Almighty God. A stark reminder of the transient nature of earthly authority."

"That doesn't seem specific to our times," I interject. "Does the Book of Revelation reveal anything about our current predicament?"

Brother Taizé takes a deep breath, centering himself. "Revelation, with its vivid and often terrifying imagery, speaks of a world in tumult. It foretells the rise of the Antichrist, the battle of Armageddon, and the triumphant return of the Messiah to restore order. It's a message of hope amid chaos, a reminder that divine justice prevails even in darkness."

Ariela leans closer, earnest curiosity filling her voice. "What do you believe? Do you think these prophecies are coming to pass?"

Brother Taizé's gaze turns inward for a moment as if seeking guidance from above. "In this arid expanse, time feels fluid, and prophecy is often open to interpretation. Yet I believe we stand on the precipice of great change, the fulfillment of ancient promises."

"Why?" Ariela asks, her brow furrowing.

He gathers his thoughts, eyes shimmering with ardent devotion. "Look for the signs woven throughout scripture. Lawlessness, a descent into sin, and echoes of Jesus' teachings in Matthew Chapter 24 all point to our turbulent times. Yet there are even more illuminating events."

"What are they?" I prompt.

"Key signs emerge in the Book of Ezekiel," he explains, his voice imbued with gravity. "We read of the dispersed Children of Israel returning to their homeland—a land that will unite, no longer divided between two entities, Judea and Samaria. This didn't occur for thousands of years until the formation of the State of Israel."

I reflect on his words. Our journey into the desert, our encounters with danger, and now this meeting with Brother Taizé all seem orchestrated by a power greater than ourselves.

"In considering the forces surrounding this country," I ask, "are there parallels between Gog in Ezekiel, the King of the North in Daniel, and the armies in the Book of Revelation?"

Brother Taizé nods thoughtfully, his eyes brimming with knowledge. "Indeed, these ancient prophecies intertwine like threads in a cosmic tapestry. Gog in Ezekiel, the King of the North in Daniel, and the armies in Revelation all converge."

He pauses, letting his words settle. "Ezekiel's Gog, described in chapters 38 and 39, emerges as a formidable coalition of nations intent on invading the land of Israel."

I remember my conversations with Khaled and Saleh, and their understanding of Gog resonated with me.

"What about the King of the North in Daniel?" Ariela presses, eager for more.

Brother Taizé continues, his voice steady. "In Daniel, we encounter a powerful ruler known as the King of the North, who challenges God's chosen people."

He gains momentum, the conviction in his voice growing. "And in Revelation, we witness apocalyptic visions of armies gathering for the battle of Armageddon, converging upon

Jerusalem. These forces, like the King of the North and Gog, represent evil arrayed against the righteous. As this physical battle unfolds, a spiritual war rages in the unseen realm, where the Messiah emerges victorious."

"In your eyes, who is the Messiah?" Ariela asks, her tone inquisitive yet respectful.

Brother Taizé's gaze softens as he meets her eyes. "The Messiah," he replies, his voice imbued with reverence, "is the Lamb of God, the Son of God Himself. He bore the sins of the world and rose again. He is the one who will usher in the ultimate triumph of good over evil, fulfilling the promise of righteousness over sin."

"I am a Jew," Ariela asserts, her voice firm.

Brother Taizé's gaze is unwavering as he responds, "And so was Jesus Christ, the embodiment of hope and redemption. He, along with His earliest followers, who were Jews, honored their heritage, worshipped in the temple, and taught the fulfillment of the very scriptures you hold dear. The New Testament, my dear, was penned by those who loved their faith deeply, every word a testament to the divine revelation of Christ. Through Him, those of us who are gentiles have the glorious privilege of entering God's holy assembly, united under His grace."

"Many Jews see Jesus as a heretic," Ariela counters, her brow furrowed with skepticism.

"And many Jews see Jesus as their Messiah."

"Secular Jews doubt all of that and question if the Messiah is real or not."

Brother Taizé, with gentle patience, replies, "It is a common misunderstanding, but listen closely to the words of Ezekiel 38. God promises that at the culmination of history, He will reveal His glory to all nations, and they will recognize Him as Lord. This prophecy is echoed in Revelation, where the fullness of His majesty is unveiled. The Messiah comes not to dismantle, but to fulfill, to gather all of humanity into a single fold of divine love."

Ariela and I exchange glances, Brother Taizé's words sinking deep. The signs he outlines are not mere abstractions; they are the vivid echoes of ancient prophecy resonating in the reality we now experience. At that moment, I feel the gravity of our existence. The thought of an imminent Messiah, interwoven with the chaos of our world, is a concept that stirs a mix of hope and fear.

"In this era of turmoil," I ponder aloud, "what is your plan in light of all this?"

Brother Taizé looks at me, his eyes sparkling with a divine fire. "I will fulfill my calling. My mission is to pray for this world and for those who have lost their way. And I will pray specifically for you both as you continue your journey."

"Thank you," Ariela says, her voice softer now, touched by his sincerity.

As time is running, I excuse myself, allowing Ariela to continue her conversation with Brother Taizé. I walk back to my SUV, gathering food and placing it in a plastic bag. I find a box filled with provisions in the back of the robbers' truck and load it up. The thought of how Brother Taizé might view the origin of this food crosses my mind, and I decide to keep it to myself.

Returning to the spring, I hand the food to Brother Taizé. He accepts it with a serene smile and says, "God bless you for your kindness, my friend. Even in difficult times, compassion is a light that reflects the heart of Christ."

"I appreciate your words and your prayers," I reply, feeling an inexplicable warmth wash over me.

Turning to Ariela, I hand her my car keys. "We must go now. I'll drive the pickup, and you can follow me. We don't have far to travel."

"Godspeed on your journey," Brother Taizé says, his voice a gentle benediction.

As we drive away, the desert seems to echo with the promise of hope, and the presence of the Messiah feels closer than ever.

Chapter 25

I steer the robbers' pickup truck over the rugged terrain, as the vehicle groans with every bump and jolt. It's a far cry from my reliable SUV with its smooth suspension.

In my rearview mirror, I catch sight of Ariela in my SUV, trailing behind to avoid the dust clouds kicked up by the truck's rough ride. I haven't had the chance to inspect the stolen pickup yet properly—its cluttered cab and the boxes of ill-gotten goods piled high in the back remain a mystery.

My thoughts drift back to our encounter with Brother Taizé at the spring. His words linger in my mind, adding a New Testament perspective to the turmoil around us. There's something almost prophetic about his presence in this forsaken landscape, like a figure straight out of the scriptures. He hitches rides and then appears unexpectedly at archeological sites, offering wisdom and support, before vanishing into the barren wilderness.

I've offered him supplies before and once even took him to Eilat for medical care. In Eilat, walking alongside him felt surreal, as if I were with a Biblical character. Meeting him at the oasis felt like a divine appointment, and I can't help but wonder how Ariela interprets this connection. We'll have plenty of time to discuss it once we reach the safety of my cave.

With about ten kilometers left to go, I spot two vehicles parked on the roadside—a small camper and a van. The memory of the Iranian's cunning trap flashes in my mind, and instinctively, I bring the truck to a halt. Ariela skillfully maneuvers my SUV to a stop beside me.

We exit the vehicles cautiously, surveying the scene with binoculars, and then we assess the situation. One of the cars appears to be having mechanical troubles, and I see Ariela's gaze sharpen, ready for anything.

"It seems manageable," she observes, her voice low and steady. "There are four adults and two young teenagers. No obvious hiding spots for ambushers, but we must proceed with caution."

I nod, double-checking her assessment through my binoculars before suggesting, "I'll approach them in the truck. You stay back for cover in case things go sideways."

She agrees with a brief nod.

As I drive closer, I notice the individuals by the vehicles react with sudden panic, diving behind the van. Suspicion gnaws at me. Are they preparing for an ambush? I halt the truck about fifty feet away, my rifle ready as I step out, using the door as a shield.

Ariela positions my SUV behind the pickup and exits, her weapon drawn, ensuring we're both ready for any outcome. "What seems to be the trouble?" I call out, trying to keep my voice calm.

Silence hangs for a moment before a cautious voice emerges from behind one of the cars. "Who are you?"

"I'm Thomas Thornton," I respond, striving to sound reassuring. "An archaeologist. This is my friend, Ariela."

"Are you robbers?" the voice asks.

"Never," I assert, recognizing their fear. Who would ask a stranger if they were robbers?

I secure my rifle in the truck's seat, raise my hands in a gesture of peace, and step into view. Ariela remains concealed, her presence a silent reassurance.

"Do you need help?" I ask gently, stepping closer.

"Where did you get the truck?" the voice queries, laced with distrust.

"We took it from two robbers," I reply, hoping this clears the air.

"How?" comes the hesitant response.

"Let's just say they won't be bothering anyone again," I answer, shifting the focus back to them. "How did you know about the truck?"

"They robbed us and took everything we had," the voice admits, pain evident in their tone.

"Well then," I say, determination surging within me, "come and take it back."

With caution, six figures emerge from behind the van—two men, two women, and two teenagers, a boy and a girl. One man wears a yarmulke, a sign of his Jewish faith, while the other does not.

Curiosity piqued, I ask about their ordeal. "How did you get robbed?"

They share a harrowing tale of being ambushed by a gunman on a lonely road. The assailant claimed others lurked nearby, ready to strike. Just when they thought they were done for, a second man appeared from behind a rock, intensifying their terror. They were forced to surrender everything—clothing, food, money—loading their possessions onto the truck, which I am now driving. In the end, it was only two assailants.

I offer a brief but resolute response. "Those two are now on a long walk home."

"Thank God," the man with the yarmulke breathes, relief washing over him.

Ariela steps forward from her concealed position, her rifle still ready. "Good afternoon. I'm truly sorry you had to endure such hardships."

"Please, reclaim what belongs to you," I instruct, taking charge of the situation.

The two women begin to sift through the boxes of stolen goods in the back of the pickup, passing items to the teenagers. Ariela watches vigilantly, ensuring they retrieve only their belongings. As the women find their clothing, the relief on their faces is priceless.

The man with the yarmulke introduces himself as Moshe Cohen, a rabbi from Jerusalem, alongside his wife, Devorah, and their thirteen-year-old daughter, Hannah. The other man, Gabriel Touma, hails from Nazareth and introduces his wife, Tabitha, and their fourteen-year-old son, Shadi. Gabriel's Hebrew has a slight accent that piques my curiosity, but I can't quite place it.

"Why are you two traveling together?" I ask, intrigued by their unexpected alliance.

Surprisingly, they explain that they met just two days ago, bonding over their shared goal of seeking safety in this treacherous landscape.

Devorah approaches us and says, "Thank you for returning our clothing and food. We were in despair. Unfortunately, our money is gone."

"Your money?" I asked, suddenly realizing I hadn't searched the truck's cab.

I head over to the truck, searching under the passenger seat and uncovering a wooden box. Opening it, I find it filled with thousands of Israeli shekels. Bringing it to the women, I say, "Please take exactly what is yours and leave the rest."

They begin counting out stacks of shekels, leaving a significant amount in the box. I can only trust their honesty. I can't help but wonder how long the shekel will retain its value in this world. Thankfully, I have the metal box of gold coins and jewelry stashed in my SUV.

As the sun beats down and the oppressive heat weighs on us, there's little time for lengthy conversation. We know the Quds Force operatives and other hostiles remain in the area. "Where are you headed?" I ask, sensing urgency.

Moshe exchanges a glance with Gabriel before answering. "While we don't know each other very well, our objectives align—we're seeking a safe place."

Gabriel nods in agreement, adding, "But we don't know where that safe place is."

His question hangs heavy in the air. In this ruthless landscape, where does safety truly lie? And I find myself facing a dilemma.

Chapter 26

As Moshe and Gabriel huddle over the camper's engine, adjusting a few loose wires, I signal Ariela to join me in my SUV. The interior feels like a sanctuary, a brief reprieve from the chaos outside where we can speak freely without the travelers overhearing.

"What's your impression of them?" I ask quietly.

Ariela leans back in her seat, her eyes drifting toward the travelers. "The two women seem honest," she begins thoughtfully. "It seems they took only what was rightfully theirs. But they also appear naive, ill-prepared for the harshness of this desert. Their fear of the impending war is obvious, but we still know very little about their past or what brought them to this remote place."

I furrow my brow, weighing her words. "Can we trust them?" I press.

She responds cautiously, "I think so, at least as much as anyone can be trusted in these unsafe times."

Contemplating our next move, I ask. "Do we just leave them to fend for themselves?"

Ariela meets my gaze, her expression reflecting the gravity of the situation. "I understand," she acknowledges. "Left alone, they're unlikely to survive in this harsh place, especially with the Quds Force and other dangers lurking around."

"I have the same concerns." I pause, reflecting on our skills as a duo. "Together, you and I can navigate this terrain. I know it well, and your military training brings another layer of strength. But they will slow us down."

Ariela turns her attention to the travelers, who are busy arranging their recovered belongings. "How much water do you have in your secret cave?" she asks.

"The last two times I visited, the water had a steady trickle, enough to sustain us all. But I can't be sure if it's seasonal."

"And what about food?" she inquires.

I offer her a reassuring smile. "I stocked enough dried goods to last me three months. Plus, we have some dates and figs. So, we should manage at least a month and a half together. But we have no idea how much food they've salvaged or what's hidden in the back of this truck. We might be able to find more supplies in Eilat."

Ariela falls into a thoughtful silence, her mind processing the options ahead. Finally, she speaks with resolve, "The right thing to do is to help them. Can we take them to your cave, at least for now? It would give them access to water and natural shelter. Once there, they can figure out their next steps."

I nod in agreement, feeling a shared purpose form between us. "Alright, let's do it," I affirm, knowing this decision implies additional responsibilities.

We exit the SUV and walk back to where Moshe and Gabriel are securing the camper's hood. Gabriel looks up, a glimmer of relief on his face. "It was just a loose wire from the bumpy road," he explains.

"That's a relief," I reply. "But there's something else we need to discuss. Ariela and I have been talking, and we'd like to extend our help. We can take you to a place with a water source and some natural protection. It will give you time to rest and decide your next steps."

Gabriel exchanges a few words with Moshe, and they form small huddles with their families. I catch Gabriel's family switching to a language I don't recognize—neither Hebrew nor Arabic. After a brief discussion, they return to us, their expressions imbued with a shared determination.

"We are grateful for your offer and would like to go with you," Moshe states earnestly.

"Us too," Gabriel adds, nodding firmly.

Within minutes, we organize a makeshift caravan, spacing our vehicles apart to minimize the dust clouds. I take the lead in the stolen truck, with Gabriel's family in the camper behind me, Moshe's family in the van, and Ariela bringing up the rear in my SUV.

As we approach the ancient wash leading to my concealed cave, I feel pressure. With each bump in the road, I am acutely aware of the escalating complexity of our situation. In this severe landscape, our fates are now intertwined.

I glance back, and my SUV is far in the rear. Knowing that Ariela is there gives me strength. Whatever awaits us in the cave, I know that together, we can face it. Somehow, amid uncertainty, there is hope—and I sense we are being guided by someone greater than ourselves.

Chapter 27

It has been an exhausting trek from Jerusalem to Be'er Sheva, and now we approach my secret cave. It's a sanctuary that now feels less private than I had hoped. Ariela and six others are with me, which stirs an unease. Since Debbie left, I've grown used to solitude, so sharing this refuge with so many feels daunting.

Our convoy winds through a narrow canyon and into a broad clearing with ample space for our vehicles. The towering brown hills form a natural fortress around us. Among these sunbaked mounds, a prominent hill to the south stands sentinel over our newfound haven.

Beyond the rocky terrain, hidden within a narrow draw, lies my cave. It shelters the life-giving water we need. Just beyond it is a valley-like area, dotted with thriving sagebrush. I suspect the plants draw moisture from the same underground spring that feeds our water source.

I instruct the group to spread out, assigning each family a designated area for privacy. Gabriel and his wife, Tabitha, set up a bed for their son, Shadi, under the awning of their camper. It provides welcome relief from the sun. Moshe's van has a compact double mattress and a fold-down bed for their daughter, Hannah. Though cramped, we all know adaptability is key.

I relinquish my two-man tent to Ariela and set up my sleeping quarters nearby. It feels strange having so many people in such close quarters, especially given our limited familiarity.

Next, we establish a latrine behind a cluster of rocks. Fourteen-year-old Shadi digs the hole with enthusiasm. As each group organizes their supplies, we discover an array of items in the back of the robbers' truck: six camping chairs, a small stove, four jerry cans of gas, a tarp, and camping supplies. We find rice, noodles, and canned vegetables—enough food for over four months. I hope someone here can cook to make our meals interesting.

We need to decide if we'll cook as a group or let families fend for themselves. Organization is essential, especially if we're here for a while.

With basic needs addressed, I lead the group to my cave. Water flows gently, filling a rock basin about the size of a large sink. We set guidelines for collecting and using this precious resource.

Ariela and I take a break under the southern hill's shade, dragging two camping chairs away from the group. We need to talk about our plans.

"Everything seems in order for now," I say, scanning the group and the rugged landscape.

Ariela nods, her eyes alert. "For now, yes. But there are other things to consider."

"Agreed," I reply. "We need to assess everyone's survival skills. Some may need guidance."

"We also need to understand why they came to the desert and what their plans are," she adds.

I see that Ariela views us as a team, which comforts me. "Knowing their backgrounds and skills could help us survive."

Concerned, she says, "There are dangers around us. Security must be a priority. We should distribute firearms to the adults and establish a defense plan."

Her suggestion is serious. "You should lead that."

Ariela hesitates. "I'd prefer they don't know my background. It's better if you lead the defense plan. I can help with weapon training but not reveal my skills."

"Why not?" I ask, already suspecting the reason. Ariela, or rather Esti Yitzhak, is the Prime Minister's daughter, trained in elite counterterrorism.

"I was instructed to go into hiding," she says quietly.

"I understand," I reply. Her capture would cause major problems for her father and the government.

"How should we present you?" I ask.

"Can I pass as an archaeologist?" she suggests.

"That might be a stretch," I smile.

"No, really. Could I?" she insists.

"Sure, let's play it by ear. If any archaeology questions come up, I'll handle them."

"And we'll say we're colleagues and friends," she continues. "Actually, let's say we're engaged. That would give me better cover."

Her proposal surprises me. "I'm not sure what 'engaged or something like that' looks like, but I'll try. You need to lead this."

"I will," she says confidently. "It won't be difficult."

"Okay," I agree, feeling the new complexities. But I understand her need to blend in and hide her identity.

We shift to the bigger picture. "To understand our situation, we need to know the state of the war. Once everyone is settled, we should go to Eilat. It's only thirty minutes away, and we can scout for supplies."

Ariela nods. "I'll check in with my headquarters. They might have important updates; my organization has a facility in Eilat."

As we focus on immediate challenges, an unspoken bond forms—a connection built during our three-day journey together. Though we tread carefully, it's a bond that can't be ignored.

Chapter 28

As the sun sets, its fading rays stretch across the desert, casting shadows on the rocky terrain. Our small group of eight sits in a circle on mismatched camping chairs salvaged from a pickup truck. We exchange wary glances.

In this strange setting, I understand the urgency of knowing who we are and why we've ended up here. I take a deep breath and decide to lead. Trust and understanding will be our lifelines in this harsh wilderness.

"It's strange how we've ended up in this situation," I begin, my voice steady as darkness envelops us. "Not long ago, we were all living our normal lives, and now we find ourselves here, united by fate in the heart of the desert."

My gaze settles on Moshe, whose yarmulke signifies his deep connection to his faith. "Could you share a bit about yourselves and what brought you here?"

Moshe clears his throat, his expression earnest. "I'm Moshe Cohen, and this is my wife, Devorah, and our daughter, Hannah. We belong to the Conservative Movement, and I teach at a yeshiva in Jerusalem."

I press further, intrigued. "What compelled you to seek refuge here?"

"The war, of course. I hold God's word to be true, and I believe in the prophecy of Zechariah 14:1-2. It foretells a day of reckoning, a time when Jerusalem will be besieged, and half the city will face exile. I believe that day is upon us," Moshe responds, conviction in his voice.

"May I respectfully ask if that prophecy wasn't already fulfilled during the destruction of the Second Temple in 70 A.D. or during the Bar Kokhba revolt in 132 A.D.?" I challenge gently.

Moshe nods. "You know your history. Those are examples of destruction, but this time feels different. We're surrounded by a coalition of nations unlike any before. After discussing it with Devorah and Hannah, we decided to take the yeshiva's van and leave."

"Thank you for sharing. Do you have experience living in the desert?"

"Next to none," he admits. "But we're eager to learn. And we shouldn't overlook the verses in Zechariah that promise God will defend Jerusalem. We hold firm to that promise."

Ariela interjects with an essential question. "Do you know how to handle a rifle?"

"No, why do you ask?" Moshe's brow furrows in confusion.

"This area can be dangerous, as you've already seen. We'll equip you with firearms and teach you how to defend yourselves," I explain, recalling Ariela's earlier guidance.

Moshe exchanges looks with Devorah and Hannah before nodding with determination. "I understand, and I'm willing to learn."

Ariela turns to Devorah. "Can you learn about weapons too? We all need to be prepared. This is reminiscent of the early days of Israel when women in the kibbutzim fought alongside the men."

"I'm willing. The memory of those robbers is still fresh in my mind," Devorah responds resolutely.

Next, I focus on Gabriel and his family. "Could you share more about yourselves?"

Gabriel, embodying quiet strength, begins. "We are Aramean. I work as a mechanic, my wife Tabitha bakes bread, and our son Shadi excels in an advanced school program in math and science. We're fluent in Aramaic, Arabic, and Hebrew. I served in the IDF."

"Have you spent much time in the desert?" I inquire.

"We enjoy camping, usually at the Kinneret, the Sea of Galilee. Most of our adventures have been in the north, where the climate is milder. We've encountered the desert, but not extensively," Gabriel reflects.

"You'll adapt and learn. Regarding your IDF service, do you have experience with rifles?" I ask.

"I served for two years and carried a rifle," Gabriel nods.

"Can you help instruct the others on firing a weapon and strategizing a defense perimeter for our camp?" I suggest.

"I can do that. We can start tomorrow," he affirms.

"What motivated you to leave your home and come here?" I ask.

"Our motivations align with Moshe's. The Book of Revelation speaks of nations converging for a great battle in the valley near

Megiddo. Nazareth sits on the eastern edge of that valley. We believe we are witnessing the signs leading up to that event, which is terrifying," Gabriel explains.

"We are driven by faith and the urgency of impending danger. For me, it's a command from Jesus to flee when armies surround Jerusalem. As you've gleaned, I'm an archaeologist with experience in this harsh land," I say.

When it's Ariela's turn, she speaks. "I'm from Tel Aviv, secular, *hiloni,* and I'm not particularly versed in prophecies. I enjoy some Jewish rituals, like lighting candles on Hanukkah, but I'm an archaeologist and the partner of Thomas—that's why I'm here."

Her words linger, heavy with unspoken meaning. Our relationship needs no further explanation.

Moshe eyes her with caution. I can sense his thoughts. How can a Jew be unaware of the Scriptures? For him, the Torah is the essence of Jewish identity. To be hiloni is to exist on the periphery, even more questionable given her partnership with a gentile.

"To ensure the group's safety, Ariela and I plan to travel to Eilat tomorrow for information about the war. While we're away, we'll rely on you to guard the camp. Gabriel will instruct you on weapon usage. If there's anything you need from Eilat, let us know, but supplies may be scarce," I explain.

"Where are the rifles?" Gabriel poses a practical question.

I lead them to the back of my SUV and reveal our modest arsenal. As I distribute rifles to the adults, Gabriel receives extra magazines and boxes of ammunition. Their expressions mix surprise with understanding.

"Where did you acquire these weapons?" Moshe's voice breaks the silence, underscoring the gravity of our situation.

"From people we encountered on our journey, some of whom weren't friendly," I respond soberly.

"Can you give one to Shadi?" Gabriel asks.

"Are you sure?"

"Yes," he insists.

I hand a rifle to Shadi, watching his eyes brighten. A wave of discomfort washes over me; something about this feels wrong. Isn't there something against child soldiers? Though Shadi isn't

Jewish, in this world, a thirteen-year-old is often viewed as an adult. Our situation is exceptional, yet this decision unsettles me.

As night falls, we retreat to our makeshift sleeping quarters. The wilderness hides dangers we can hardly fathom. I spread my sleeping bag on a pad near Ariela's tent, surrounded by the eerie silence of the night. I wonder how long this stillness will last.

Chapter 29

The drive from our campsite to Eilat takes roughly thirty minutes, and Ariela and I set off early in the morning. As we leave the group behind, they wave us off, and I hope they don't feel abandoned. The straight, smooth desert road gives us an opportunity to converse.

"What do you think of our group?" I ask, my gaze fixed on the winding road.

Ariela pauses to gather her thoughts. "Honestly, I'm not sure the two families would manage well on their own. Gabriel's mechanical skills and IDF background provide practical knowledge, which is invaluable. His son, Shadi, is intelligent and eager to help. Tabitha has culinary experience from her bakery job, and I suspect Devorah can cook as well. Then there's Hannah—sweet and naive at thirteen, caught somewhere between fantasy and reality. Moshe is determined but could use a strong hand to guide him. Overall, I believe they're in a reasonably good place for now. Still, it's too soon to tell if they can endure what's ahead."

"We'll have to take the lead," I respond, glancing at her. "Especially when it comes to building a defensive strategy."

Ariela nods in agreement, her expression steady. "Absolutely. The defending force often holds the advantage, provided they're well-prepared."

"That's your area of expertise," I say, "but I've excavated ancient city walls that have withstood sieges, so I have some insights on fortifications."

She looks at me curiously. "Do you enjoy archaeology?"

I consider her question for a moment. "I did, but lately, it's started to feel more like a routine than a passion. Maybe it had become a wall I hid behind."

Ariela leans in, her voice gentle as she asks, "In what way?"

I hesitate, surprised by my honesty. "It's about relationships. I've felt like a failure in that department. Work and hobbies can become convenient excuses for avoiding personal connections."

She nods knowingly. "I can relate. My job brings its challenges, making it hard to build meaningful relationships."

After a brief silence, I venture, "Is there someone special in your life right now?"

"A relationship?" she clarifies.

I nod.

Ariela sighs softly, her vulnerability evident. "Painful experiences leave scars. No, there hasn't been anyone for quite a while. My role requires me to be guarded and diplomatic, which complicates personal connections."

I feel relieved to hear her answer. "Can I ask about this unique role?"

She shifts her gaze to the passing landscape and breathes deeply. "I'd rather not get into that."

"Does it have anything to do with going incognito, as you mentioned before?" I inquire, sensing the sensitivity of the topic.

"Yes," she acknowledges with a nod, "but let's leave it at that for now. We need to focus on what's necessary."

"As partners?" I suggest offering a subtle overture.

A smile spreads across her face as she reaches over to pat my hand resting on the steering wheel. "Yes, I like that," she replies, the gesture infused with unspoken implications.

"Me too," I say, returning her smile. We lapse into a comfortable silence, and I consider our newfound partnership. The road ahead straightens, leading us onto a paved route toward Eilat.

Eilat, nestled on the northern shore of the Gulf of Aqaba, offers a unique vantage point overlooking the Jordanian town of Aqaba to the east. I've visited both cities multiple times and am familiar with their distinct Israeli and Arab characteristics.

The Gulf of Aqaba, typically a serene paradise, now shimmers against a backdrop of rugged terrain. The looming mountains of the Sinai Peninsula frame the horizon. In more peaceful times, Eilat thrives as a coastal haven with modern buildings, palm-lined promenades, bustling cafes, and restaurants where the aroma of Mediterranean cuisine mingles with the salty sea air. Sunbathers bask in the warmth while divers explore vibrant coral reefs teeming with marine life.

But upon our arrival, Eilat reveals a different story. Once a place of carefree enjoyment, the city now bears the scars of impending conflict. Crowds of anxious faces fill the streets, predominantly older individuals, while young and middle-aged adults have been called into military service.

As we navigate through the congested city, the transformation becomes starkly evident. Lines of worried people snake outside stores, their supplies rationed by weary shopkeepers. The usual vibrancy has been replaced by an atmosphere thick with apprehension, leaving its mark on every conversation and furrowed brow.

Ariela guides me through the heart of the city, steering north toward the Eilat airport. We turn into an industrial area and arrive at a nondescript building. A tall security fence encloses the back lot, and she instructs me to stay in the car before disappearing inside. I can only imagine the flurry of activity within— government agents exchanging critical information, maps sprawled across tables, intelligence officers piecing together the puzzle of the looming conflict.

After what feels like an eternity, Ariela returns and directs me to the back of the building. A gate opens, granting us access to a courtyard filled with parked vehicles. Two men emerge, swiftly loading my car with essential supplies: food, a shortwave radio, boxes of ammunition, and additional clothing for Ariela. The gravity of our situation weighs heavily on their stern expressions as they guide me to a gas pump and fill my tank.

With our mission complete, we leave the warehouse complex, and as we reach the edge of the city, Ariela suggests we take a break at a small coffee bar. When seated at a table, we order coffee along with plates of hummus and pita bread, seeking a moment of respite amidst the chaos. My attention, however, is drawn to a man at a nearby table, his gaze fixated on Ariela. While she's undeniably attractive, something about his demeanor sends alarm bells ringing.

Forgetting about the stranger, I turn to Ariela. "What did you find out?"

"The war has taken a dire turn," she replies.

"How so?" I ask, my concern deepening.

"Reports from the north are troubling. There's gunfire on both sides. While diplomacy is underway, the enemy continues to amass troops. Estimates suggest nearly a million soldiers are approaching from the east. In the south, armies from Libya, Egypt, and Sudan are gathering forces, along with factions from Ethiopia and several African nations."

"That's serious," I say, the frightening reality settling in.

Ariela nods, her expression grave. "Europe's involvement complicates matters further, with troops building up in Greece and Cyprus. The U.S. military is also joining the European forces."

"It's absurd when you think about it," I assert. "Do you know if the southern armies will follow the Mediterranean route, or will they move up the Red Sea and along the Gulf of Aqaba? If it's the latter, our campsite will be directly in their path."

"Yes," she agrees, "it's a sobering thought. We need a contingency plan."

Returning to the topic of her mission, I ask, "Any updates on your orders?"

Ariela shakes her head. "No, they've instructed me to stay with you. Your reputation as a friend of Israel precedes you. Dr. Peretz vouched for you, stating you're reliable and resourceful. They believe our partnership serves as solid cover."

I nod appreciatively. "That's reassuring." The thought that someone had been monitoring me is unsettling, but anyone accompanying the Prime Minister's daughter would naturally attract scrutiny.

The man who had been watching Ariela rises from his table, heading for his car. His gaze meets ours one last time before he leaves, leaving behind an unsettling feeling.

"A man was watching you," I say, concern creeping into my voice. "He's over there." I point toward the parking lot.

Ariela glances at the man as he walks away. "Israeli men often check out women," she remarks casually.

"It felt different," I insist. "There was something off about him."

Ariela nods in agreement. "We should go."

We return to my SUV and head west toward our camp, our minds racing with the knowledge of the impending threat from the south and the pressing need to devise a plan.

Chapter 30

As I drive westward, the sun blazes directly onto my front windscreen, heating the car like an oven. Turning on the air conditioning feels like a betrayal—each drop of gas is precious, a luxury we can't afford. Instead, I roll down all the windows, letting the dry wind whip through the vehicle, feeling its aridity press against my skin.

Just before we reach the dry riverbed leading to our camp, I catch sight of two pickups in the distance, their silhouettes wavering in the heat waves rising from the parched earth. An uneasy feeling coils in my stomach. I glance over at Ariela, my steadfast companion on this treacherous journey. She's already preparing her rifle, her movements methodical and precise. The flicker of apprehension in her eyes betrays her calm demeanor.

In the back of one truck, a tarp forms a makeshift mountain, and crammed within it are four goats, their bleats muted by the oppressive heat. As the vehicles approach, recognition washes over me like a sudden storm, and I feel a surge of mixed emotions—relief, worry, and a sense of responsibility. Instinctively, I pull over to the roadside and say to Ariela, "They don't pose a threat."

Still, she keeps her weapon ready, her vigilance a reminder of the precariousness of our situation.

The trucks slow down, their engines settling into a low, rumbling growl that reverberates through the oppressive landscape. I spot Khalid in the first truck, worry etched into his weathered face. Beside him are his wife and young daughter, their eyes anxious. In the second truck, Salem—a man of few words— sits in the driver's seat, his wife beside him. I realize I don't even know the names of the women.

I wave, and when Khalid sees me, a flicker of recognition and relief crosses his features. We get out of our vehicles, and I extend a firm, reassuring handshake to both Khalid and Salem. Their wives remain in the trucks, as does Ariela, who I know is still gripping her rifle tightly. The greeting flows naturally from our lips.

"*As-salamu alaykum*," I say, the words a ritual greeting, one I hope brings some measure of peace.

"*Wa alaykum as-salam*," Khalid replies, his voice steady, though his eyes betray his fears.

Ariela peers through the windscreen, confusion knitting her brow at the warmth exchanged between us. The warmth feels foreign in this new reality, a stark reminder of the dividing lines now drawn by conflict and fear.

"How has your journey been?" I ask, invoking the ancient tradition of desert travelers.

Khalid's face falls. "We have experienced troubles," he begins, his voice trembling slightly. "Quds Force, the terrorists, visited us again, and they were hostile. They threatened us, demanding we turn against Israelis. They don't seem to realize we are Israelis ourselves. They threatened our wives with things unthinkable. This forced us into a nightmarish position. We packed up and left, driven by fear and necessity."

"What were the reasons, if I may ask?" I urge, desperate to understand the full extent of their ordeal.

"Besides their threats, we were running out of water," Khalid admits, his eyes scanning the horizon as if searching for hope. "We decided to move closer to Eilat, thinking Israeli soldiers might offer us protection. But with the war, Eilat might not be safe anymore."

His words remind me of the unpredictable danger surrounding us. I feel an urgent need to dig deeper, grasp the reality of their situation, and find a way to help this desperate family. "Where are you planning to go?" I ask, my voice tinged with concern.

Khalid's brow furrows. "We're not sure yet," he confesses. "We need to find a water source."

I nod solemnly. "Give me a minute," I say, stepping away from them to beckon Ariela, who exits our car with her rifle slung over her shoulder. We huddle together, whispering about the harsh reality of their situation.

"I remember them," Ariela says. "They're from the Bedouin camp where the Quds Force operatives were staying."

I nod, unease creeping in. "But those Bedouins weren't actively supporting the Quds Force. They were hospitable to me, even welcoming me into their tent for tea." I glance back at the two pickup trucks. "We could use their expertise in desert survival."

Ariela's gaze sharpens, her protective instincts flaring. "But can we trust them?" she asks.

I consider her question carefully, weighing the risks against the potential benefits. "I believe so," I assert, my eyes drawn back to Khalid and Salem. "Plus, their brother serves in the IDF. Our goal is survival, Ariela. The people in our camp lack the necessary skills. If the enemy army to the south attacks, we need all the help we can get."

Ariela takes a moment. Finally, she concedes, her voice filled with reluctant agreement. "Okay, I agree."

We approach Khalid and Salem, the gravity of the moment weighing heavily on my shoulders. "You need a water source, and we have one near a secret spring," I say, my voice steady but urgent. "It's a safe place for now. There are already two other families there. Would you be willing to join us? You are very welcome."

Khalid and Salem exchange glances, their eyes reflecting a mixture of gratitude and hesitation. The silence stretches thick with unspoken fears until Salem nods, and Khalid's voice finally breaks through. "Yes," he says, relief evident in his tone. "We'd be grateful to share your camp."

With the decision made, we all climb back into our vehicles. Khalid and Salem maneuver their trucks expertly, following us toward the turnoff that leads to our camp.

As we arrive, the other families emerge to greet us. Their initial surprise at the sight of two pickup trucks—and the presence of Bedouin strangers—is intense. Moshe's eyes narrow with suspicion. But Gabriel, ever the diplomat, steps forward, offering a warm welcome in Arabic to the newcomers.

I introduce Khalid and Salem, who present their wives, Hala and Rana, and Khalid's daughter, Layla. The awkwardness hangs in the air, a collision of cultures and backgrounds that feels almost tangible. The Bedouins, accustomed to navigating such encounters, choose to set up their tents in an open area, intentionally distancing themselves from the rest of the campers.

Shadi and Hannah are immediately drawn to the goats, and a few moments later, they happily converse in Hebrew with Khalid's young daughter. They lead the goats through the gap to the open space beyond where shrubs offer food for the animals, their laughter a brief reprieve in the heaviness of the moment.

As evening descends, we gather for a communal dinner, knowing the outside world is an entirely different place than our fragile sanctuary. Ariela and I take center stage, sharing the information we gathered in Eilat. I emphasize the growing threat of war, the ominous presence of the army in the south, and my growing responsibility.

The Bedouin families, in turn, share their own harrowing experiences, revealing that their brother serves in the IDF, stationed in the south. Bedouins in the IDF are invaluable scouts, and their intimate understanding of the desert terrain is an asset in these dire times.

Seizing the moment, I ask Khalid and Salem if they might be willing to teach the rest of us their survival skills. The urgency in my voice echoes the heavy burden I bear. "We may need to relocate swiftly as the war unfolds," I caution, the stakes clearer than ever.

Salem responds, "We are not teachers, but if you live with us, you will learn our customs and ways, and we will learn from you. For Moshe, Gabriel, and your families, this may be a way to connect with our patriarch, Ibrahim, who existed on this land. Living in a barren region is in our blood."

"Thank you," Moshe says, his voice steady.

As darkness envelops the camp, I retreat to my sleeping area. The arrival of the Bedouins adds more complexity. Relaxation feels like a distant memory, a luxury that eludes me.

Before Ariela heads to her tent, she walks over to me. "Thank you for driving to Eilat today. I'm grateful for everything you're doing," she says, sincerity in her eyes.

"I'm not doing much," I reply, feeling a wave of humility.

"Actually, you are. You provide leadership and comfort to others and companionship to me. It's what I need—or should I say, what I've been missing."

I hesitate, words caught in my throat, and finally say, "I feel the same about you."

"We will survive this together," she states firmly.

Then she steps closer, wrapping her arms around me in a warm embrace that momentarily disarms the stress. I feel her heartbeat against my chest, and in that moment, we stay close, sharing a fragile strength and comfort. The entire world fades, and for just a moment, it's only us.

Breaking away, Ariela retreats to her tent. I undress and crawl into my sleeping bag, the fabric cool against my skin. But the comfort is fleeting, overshadowed by the distant hum of her shortwave radio, the voice crackling softly in the darkness. It's good that we have this connection to the outside world, even in its turmoil.

Questions spiral through my mind. Are we truly living in the end times? How will this unfold? I think of the prophecies that have haunted my thoughts. If we survive, what then? What kind of future awaits us, if any?

To make an adequate plan, I need to fit the pieces of the prophetic puzzle together—if not all of it, then at least some semblance of clarity. Each fragment feels slippery and elusive, taunting me with the enormity of the task ahead.

This secret cave and spring, which had once been my idealistic haven—a sanctuary where I could escape the world's chaos—now feels like a gilded cage. I'm struck by the realization that this may not be the best place for us anymore. The thrill of survival has turned into a sobering acknowledgment of our vulnerability.

In the solitude of my thoughts, I reflect on the bonds we've formed with Khalid and his family, the fragile ties that tether us to one another in this stark environment. The world outside may be chaotic, but here, in this shared space, we have the chance to create something meaningful amidst the turmoil.

I close my eyes, and for a moment, I allow myself to imagine a future beyond this war. A future where we are not just surviving but thriving, where children laugh and play, where the desert blooms with life instead of death. It's a fleeting vision, but it lingers, filling me with a stubborn resolve to fight for that possibility.

As I drift off to sleep, the darkness swallows me, but my mind remains restless, filled with thoughts of the challenges ahead and the uncertain road that lies before us. Yet, in the depths of despair, there's a spark of hope—a belief that we can endure, that together, we can find a way through the storm.

Chapter 31

As dawn breaks, the camp awakens to the soft glow of the morning light, each member stirring with a blend of hope and apprehension about the day's unfamiliar prospects. The first thing that caught my eye was Hala and Rana's vibrant clothing. They wear traditional dresses woven from light, colorful fabrics adorned with sequins that catch the sunlight. The colors pop against the subtle browns and reds of the surrounding hills, infusing our small group with a richness that is both refreshing and profound. Their attire reflects a culture that, though foreign, brings a unique diversity worthy of appreciation.

Rana's voice rises in a lovely Bedouin song, its melodic notes wrapping around us like a warm embrace, transporting our minds to a time when life was simple and serene. The beauty of her song contrasts sharply with our current reality.

Ariela emerges from her tent, her expression heavy with the burden of the night's vigil spent listening to the radio's grim updates. She approaches me, urgency in her stride. "I have some news," she begins, her voice laden with the gravity of what she's learned. "The armies from the south are taking two routes to Israel," she explains, her brow furrowing with concern. "One combined force from Egypt, Libya, and Algeria is advancing along the Mediterranean coastal route, gathering in the Sinai Desert at a town called Bir Qatia. They could reach our border in less than two hours. But there's another army, composed of Sudanese troops and factions from Ethiopia and elsewhere, mobilizing at Sharm El-Sheikh, about two hundred and thirty kilometers south of Eilat. That one worries me most."

The severity of the situation sinks in, a chill racing down my spine. "That's a direct violation of the Israel-Egypt Sinai Agreement from 1979," I reply, my voice steady. "Egypt agreed that only their border guards and police would be stationed in the Sinai. The presence of these armies breaks the treaty. If they're moving from Sharm El-Sheikh, it's safe to assume they have their sights set on us."

Ariela nods solemnly, her gaze unwavering. "Diplomacy may be in play, but the real question is whether the IDF will act first or wait for these troops to advance further north. A full-scale war could erupt at any moment, and we could find ourselves caught in the middle."

My thoughts drift to Zevi Yitzhak, the Prime Minister, burdened with the immense pressure of these trying times. Yet, there's something more immediate to address. "So, what should we do?" I ask, seeking clarity.

She searches my eyes, clearly grappling with the enormity of our situation. "I don't know," she admits. "Can you gather the group? They look to you as their leader."

"Okay," I reply, aware of the responsibility of leadership. Sure, I've led a few archaeological digs, but this is different. This type of leadership demands confidence and vision. What's more intimidating is knowing that people's lives are on the line.

We share a quick meal of instant oatmeal topped with chopped dates and figs. Afterward, Arial sets off to gather the others, leaving me to contemplate the uncertain road ahead.

Thirty minutes later, all ten adults are seated in a shaded area by the cliff, each in their camping chairs. Khalid and Saleh's wives are present but slightly uncomfortable; their culture typically reserves strategic discussions for men.

I gesture for Ariela to update everyone on the war and its implications for our group. Her words resonate with gravity, a somber cloud hanging over us as we absorb the implications of her report.

Once everyone is listening, I pose the critical question: "What should we do? Do we stay here, risking the arrival of the enemy army from the south, or do we act? In this moment of decision, perhaps we should reevaluate why we came here in the first place. We all assumed signs pointed to the end times based on our holy texts. But is that enough to determine our fate? I propose we look to our scriptures for guidance. Is there insight to be found?"

To my surprise, Khalid breaks the silence. "We discussed this with Thomas before," he begins, his voice steady with conviction. "Our holy book tells us that before the day of resurrection, Gog and Magog will be released, rushing from every slope. It's one of the major signs of the end times, followed by the blowing of the trumpet and the onset of the Day of Judgment. Other than that, we are instructed to repent for our sins. But I'm not a scholar of the Quran, so there may be more we're missing."

Saleh nods in agreement, reinforcing his brother's words. "Khalid is right. We know that this final battle is approaching, and it seems to be upon us because of Gog's advance."

"Thank you both," I acknowledge their insights, feeling the depth of their insights. I believe that the writer of the Quran sourced ideas from the Old Testament, but I don't want to start a theological debate at this point. "Does anyone else have anything to add?"

Moshe, who has been listening intently, speaks next. "What Khalid and Saleh have said is intriguing, something I hadn't considered before. The Tanakh, in the Book of Daniel, mentions a terrible King of the North who will destroy Israel and other nations. Some Jewish scholars believe this king has already come, but I must disagree. In terms of our course of action, Daniel 11:41 says, 'The King of the North will invade the Beautiful Land. Many countries will fall, but Edom, Moab, and the leaders of Ammon will be delivered from his hand.' If we trust in God, then Edom could be our refuge."

I nod, absorbing this new perspective. "That's something to think about. The ancient city of Petra lies in Edom, and I've worked on archaeological digs southeast of there. I know the water sources." Turning to Gabriel, I ask, "What about insights from the New Testament?"

Gabriel ponders before responding. "There may not be explicit instructions, but Jesus warned that when armies surround Jerusalem, it signals its desolation is near. He urged those in Judea to flee to the mountains. In the Book of Revelation, a woman flees to the wilderness for three and a half years, nourished during her time there. We understand this woman represents either Israel or members of the Christian church. What we know is that a spiritual battle is occurring, and Jesus will reveal himself and judge the living and the dead."

Khalid speaks out. "You are wrong. It is Allah who will judge."

Gabriel's eyes narrow, and before a full-fledged religious debate erupts, I raise my hand and say, "Let's just share our understandings."

Khalid and Gabriel sit back, but I see they want to argue their points.

Their understanding of these prophecies leaves uncertainties as I contemplate our next steps. "It appears we have specific prophecies but no clear roadmap. Would Devorah, Tabitha, Hala, or Rana like to share anything?" I ask, hoping to hear from the wives.

Hala, the young mother and wife of Khalid, hesitates, clearly uncomfortable but determined. "To speak of venturing further into the desert is a profound invitation for a Bedouin. Despite the hardships, it is a place of peace where the soul finds renewal. I've discovered that the desert is where beauty and spirituality intertwine, where angels whisper among the hills and mountains, where Moses heard the voice of the All-Powerful. At night, the stars reveal the majesty of divine creation. We can flee from the coming destruction, but it is much more than that. I will support Khalid and the rest of you if you make this decision."

Khalid's face lights up with pride as he hears Hala take this initiative.

"Thank you, Hala," I say. Turning to Ariela, I ask, "What do you think?"

Ariela smiles softly. "Hala expressed that beautifully. It adds a new dimension to our discussion. I'd like to see what the group decides."

I turn to the others. "Given that armies surround Israel, do we all agree that Edom should be our destination?"

A spirited discussion ensues, the wives actively participating, creating a chorus of voices in Hebrew, Arabic, and Aramaic. Eventually, as the debate winds down, the married couples unanimously confirm that Edom should be our refuge and that we must leave as soon as possible. We will take the prophecy literally.

Ariela brings the meeting to a close. "Let's go."

Yet practical questions linger unanswered. The scriptures may guide our faith, but they don't provide detailed instructions for survival in a harsh environment, cut off from resources and supplies. We're taking a leap of faith, trusting that God, who once provided manna in the wilderness, will watch over us.

As the group disperses to prepare for our imminent departure, my thoughts drift back to the promise of the Messiah's coming. This promise feels almost too extraordinary to believe, hanging in the air like a fragile hope as we busily pack our belongings.

Then, an unexpected interruption shatters the quiet morning. Shadi bursts into the campsite, his face a mask of fear. "Men are coming—six of them—and they carry guns."

Chapter 32

Shadi's words hit like a jolt, snapping us out of our false sense of calm. My heart pounds as questions flood my mind—who are these intruders, and how did they find us here? There's no time for answers.

Gabriel's voice is sharp, urgent, slicing like a blade. "Take your positions.

Gabriel had trained them in a defense plan. I pray it's enough. In a flurry of motion, Moshe, Devorah, Gabriel, and Tabitha dart to their vehicles, retrieving their rifles with practiced efficiency.

Shadi, holding his rifle, trembles. His face is pale, eyes wide with fear. He's just a kid—too young for this. Guilt squeezes my chest as I motion him over. "Shadi, come here," I say softly, taking the rifle from his shaking hands.

His disappointment is obvious, but I can't let him shoulder this burden. "You have a more important job," I say firmly. "Take the kids to where you feed the goats. Hide. Keep them safe."

Reluctantly, he nods, calling Hannah and Layla as they scurry toward the rocks. The goats remain tied to stakes by Khalid's truck, oblivious to the bedlam around them.

I turn to Khalid and Salem, who stand resolutely with their wives. My mind races through options. "Can either of you shoot?" I ask, my voice hard.

"I can," Salem steps forward, determined. I hand him Shadi's rifle.

"Go to Ariela. She'll give you a position."

I spin toward my SUV, retrieve my handgun, and give it to Khalid. "Get Hala, Rana, and join the kids. Stay with Shadi." He takes the weapon without a word, understanding dawning in his eyes.

As they disappear into the rocky landscape, I sprint to join Ariela, who is crouched behind a massive boulder. The path ahead narrows into a canyon, the only way in or out of our camp—both a fortress and a trap. Together, we peer down at the road.

Six men come into view. No uniforms, just rugged clothes—jeans, t-shirts, boots—but their weapons are serious, likely AK-

47s. My stomach churns. Are we ready for this? Have we trained enough? Are they friends or foes?

My voice erupts instinctively in Hebrew. "What do you want?"

The response is instant—bullets scream through the air, striking the rock with a vicious crack. I flinch as shards of stone cut across my face. There's no mistaking their intent. They're here to kill us.

Ariela fires back without hesitation. From my vantage point, I see one man crumple to the ground. The rest scatter for cover along the roadside. Gunfire echoes in every direction, a deadly orchestra. Moshe breaks from cover, his shots wild and uncontrolled, missing their targets. My heart tightens—he's too exposed, too inexperienced.

Gabriel and Salem, though, are steady. Their shots are calculated and precise. Another attacker falls. Ariela waits, breathing slowly, and fires a single shot—another enemy drops.

Chaos surrounds us. The attackers' bullets ricochet off the rocks, and I see one lining up a shot at Devorah. Time slows as I raise my rifle, steady my aim, and squeeze the trigger. The man stumbles, hit squarely in the chest, his rifle clattering to the ground.

But there's no time to process what I've done. Gunfire still rages. Then, suddenly, there's a shift. One by one, the attackers are falling. With only two remaining, they exchange desperate signals, realizing their mission is failing.

I see them retreating, but one pauses, turning to aim in my direction. Before I can react, Ariela, Gabriel, and Salem fire in unison. The man drops, joining the other lifeless forms below. The last attacker stumbles and a final volley brings him down.

Silence. An eerie, oppressive silence falls over the canyon, broken only by the wind. My heart still pounds, my mind racing, grappling with the aftermath. Slowly, I make my way down the hill, Ariela by my side. The others watch from their positions, vigilant, rifles still in hand.

Six bodies lie sprawled across the earth, their lifeless forms a chilling reminder of how close we came to death. We start searching their pockets, finding fake Israeli IDs, shekels, and car keys—clues, but no answers. Ariela's eyes narrow as she examines one of the attackers.

"We saw him yesterday at the roadside restaurant near Eilat," she says, voice tight with realization.

I glance at the ID card. "A collaborator. He must have tracked us here."

Ariela nods grimly. "This ID isn't fake. I need to send it to our contacts in Eilat. We might be able to uncover more—maybe find other collaborators."

We climb back up to the others, where relief mingles with fear in their eyes. Gabriel and Salem keep watch over the road while Devorah and Tabitha exchange silent glances, their faces pale but resolute.

"You did well," I say, my voice hoarse. "We survived."

Moshe's eyes are wide, his face still reflecting the horror of what just happened. "I never thought I'd have to do that," he mutters.

Ariela steps forward, placing a hand on Devorah and Tabitha's shoulders. "You were brave. We all were."

There's no time to dwell on it. "Pack up," I order. "We need to move."

We scramble to break down camp, loading our vehicles with hurried efficiency. The desert wind howls through the canyon as we work, every second feeling like a countdown to another attack.

Just as we're about to leave, my truck taken from the robbers won't start. Panic flares in my chest. Gabriel rushes over, throwing open the hood. Every second feels like an eternity as he works. The sun bears down, making everything feel even more oppressive. Finally, the engine coughs to life.

We move, passing the fallen bodies of our enemies as we drive out of the canyon. There's no time for sympathy or remorse, just survival.

When we reach the wash leading to the dirt road, I spot two new trucks parked and loaded with supplies. The realization hits—this was more than an attack. These men had resources, and their mission was well-funded. But now, these trucks were ours.

"Let's make an exchange," I suggest.

Saleh grins, and we move quickly, transferring goods from his battered vehicle to the newer trucks. Soon, our convoy is ready—Moshe's van, Gabriel's camper, Khalid's truck, and two fresh vehicles. Ariela leads in my SUV, and we head toward Eilat. But even as we drive, my thoughts race ahead, beyond the horizon. The enemy to the south is still out there, looming. We're not safe yet. Not by a long shot.

Chapter 33

The road to Eilat stretches ahead, a ribbon of cracked dirt meandering through the barren landscape. Our small convoy is a scattered formation, each vehicle maintaining a safe distance to avoid the thick curtain of dust kicked up by those ahead. I find myself driving the second of the two new trucks we've acquired from the Quds Force, a world of difference between the robbers' truck that groaned with each tiny bump in the road. It's a formidable machine, but my heart longs for the familiarity of my SUV just ahead and the comforting presence of Ariela beside me.

As we drive, I'm left alone with my thoughts. The adrenaline from the recent firefight still courses through my veins. Facing off against seasoned terrorists was a harrowing experience, one that will leave a lasting memory. I can't help but admire the courage displayed by every member of our group.

My mind drifts to the remarkable transformation that has unfolded over the past few days, from the quiet life of an unassuming archaeologist to a leader entrusted with the lives of twelve individuals.

Each member of our diverse crew possesses unique talents. Gabriel has proven himself invaluable not just with his mechanical skills but as a trainer in the art of combat. Salem, despite his soft-spoken nature, demonstrated unflinching bravery in the face of danger. Devorah and Tabitha's efficiency in camp life and culinary prowess offer comfort amidst the chaos. They were brave to stand on that ridge with the others. Hala and Rana, our mysterious Bedouin companions, hold untold wisdom about surviving in this severe territory. I'm sure we can learn from them. Shadi is an intelligent young guy, and the two younger girls, Hannah and Layla, bring innocence and life to the camp.

My thoughts dwell on the myriad possibilities Edom offers. It's an expansive region spanning from the Dead Sea to the Gulf of Aqaba in modern-day southwest Jordan. Among its historical gems is Petra, an ancient city sculpted from rock by the Nabateans around 400 B.C. To the west lies Jabal Haroun, a mountain considered sacred by Muslims, Christians, and Jews, who believe it to be the resting place of Aaron, Moses' brother. A Byzantine monastery once crowned its summit, which is a testament to its spiritual significance. There, I once assisted in giving an analysis of some artifacts they had found when excavating the Monastery's outlying buildings.

Close by Petra is the town of Wadi Musa, known as the Valley of Moses in Arabic. Here, tourists can find rest in hotels, restaurants, and shops while visiting Petra. It's also believed to be the place where Moses miraculously brought forth water by striking a rock with his staff.

But my mind goes further eastward, to a remote and rugged area some forty kilometers from Wadi Musa. This desolate expanse has yielded over three hundred archaeological sites, spanning from the Paleolithic era to the Islamic period. Among the treasures hidden here are rock art, tombs, forts, villages, and intricate water systems. I've explored many of these sites in my years as an archaeologist, some tucked away in the most secluded corners of the region. It's an ideal place for vanishing from prying eyes.

Yet, my contemplations are abruptly interrupted by the shrill ring of my phone. It's a startling sound, considering it had been rendered mute for days following the destruction of the telephone transmission towers. It looks like telephones are now back online.

I glance at the unfamiliar number before answering hesitantly, "Hello?" I ask, bracing for more bad news.

"Hello, Thomas." Ariela's voice.

A smile tugs at the corners of my mouth. "Nice to hear your voice. How did you even get my number?"

She laughs lightly, "I have my ways. I called the intelligence service, and they gave it to me."

I blink. "Wait, are they... tracking me?"

There's a pause, then a too-casual, "Well... yes."

I sigh. "Of course, they are."

We exchange some pleasantries, the awkwardness of our recent brush with death hanging between us like unspoken words. But Ariela has a way of steering conversations exactly where she wants them to go.

"Thomas, I've been thinking," she begins, her voice a little too casual. "When we get to Eilat, I want you to take everyone to that roadside restaurant we visited before."

"I remember," I reply cautiously, wondering what angle she's working. "Why?"

"I need to visit our organization's office in the industrial zone," she says smoothly, "but I need to go alone."

I nod, understanding. This is covert stuff. "Sure, I'll handle the group. You handle... whatever secret mission you've got going on."

"Thanks," she replies, but then, after a pause, her voice softens. "Thomas, that firefight made me realize something important."

My grip on the wheel tightens. "What's that?"

"I wouldn't want to lose you," she says, and just like that, the words are out there, hovering in the air between us. "You're different from anyone I've known."

Emotions swirl in my chest. I try to think of something meaningful to say, but all I manage is, "Uh, thanks."

She laughs—light and airy. "I'm serious. You're strong, kind, and... I like the way you take charge when things get tough."

"Well, you're not so bad yourself," I quip, but I can feel my heart racing. What is this? A battlefield confession?

There's a pause, and then Ariela goes straight for the heart of it. "Thomas, what do you think of . . . our partnership?"

I blink, caught off guard. "Partnership? Well, we work well together, sure."

"No, I mean our partnership." Her voice has that same straightforward edge, the kind Israelis are known for. "I think we both felt something back there. Am I wrong?"

My mind flashes back to the hug we shared last night. It lingered, more than just a casual embrace. "I did feel something," I admit, trying to match her honesty.

"So... where do we go from here?" she asks.

"I—uh—guess we... continue the partnership?" I fumble, realizing I'm out of my depth.

Ariela laughs again, but then she turns serious. "Thomas, life is unpredictable, and our days may be numbered. I'm not the kind of person who waits around."

"Are you saying what I think you're saying?" I ask, my pulse quickening.

"I am. Thomas, I think we should get married."

"Wait—what?" I splutter, gripping the wheel like it's the only thing grounding me to reality. "Marriage? As in, marriage-marriage?"

"Do you have a better plan?" she counters, teasing but serious. "Long engagements aren't exactly practical in our situation."

"Well, when you put it that way..." I mutter. "Sure, I mean, why not? Let's get married. No big deal."

"I'm glad we agree," Ariela says, her voice a little too calm for someone who has just proposed. "We'll figure out the details when we get to Eilat."

"You mean like how, where, and when?"

The line goes dead, leaving me sitting there in stunned silence. Have I just... agreed to get married? My mind reels. This is a new level of crazy.

The call suddenly ends, leaving me with a swirling combination of emotions. Had that conversation been real? Was she playing with my heart? I feel confused. Was that really Ariela talking? Am I ready for this? The questions linger, unanswered.

I like her, but do I love her? But what is love? Is it a fleeting emotion or something more profound based on commitment? Could I commit to Ariela at that level? I think so.

Do I want her? The answer is yes. And she got it right. Time is short.

I can hardly concentrate on the road.

As we continue our journey to Eilat, Ariela guides us to a vast gravel-covered parking lot adjacent to the familiar roadside restaurant. We pull in, one by one, parking our vehicles. Ariela goes from car to car, instructing everyone to relax, have some food, and remain here until her call comes.

Finally, she reaches my truck, a warm smile on her face as she asks, "Are you okay?"

I return her smile, my unease melting away in her presence. "Besides a strange telephone call, I'm doing fine," I admit.

"I meant it," she says, her eyes locking onto mine.

I smile back, my heart soaring. "Me too, I think. I'm not sure I know you."

Ariela leans in, her lips meeting mine in a kiss that speaks of both longing and promise. She withdraws slightly, her hands resting on the base of the open window. "Anyway, my group told me to take on a different identity, and being married to you will make a good cover story."

With that, she turns away, heading toward my SUV. A minute later, she's driving into Eilat, leaving me with a sense of confusion.

Chapter 34

On the sun-drenched terrace of the roadside restaurant, a pleasant warmth settles over us, and the scent of sizzling food mingles with the comforting aroma of spices and herbs. From where we sit, the city of Eilat glows in the distance, framed by a backdrop of desert and sea. It's one of those moments that feels oddly serene, given the chaos we left behind just this morning.

We gather at the tables, now pushed together like an impromptu family reunion, and the clinking of glasses and cutlery fills the air. Every dish brought to the table is an edible masterpiece. There's sabich with crispy eggplant, creamy tahini, and shakshuka rich with poached eggs simmered in spicy tomato sauce. Golden falafel balls practically beg to be devoured, and the schnitzel? Crispy perfection. Then there's hummus, smooth and silky, that makes you forget there's a world outside this little oasis.

The first few bites calm the collective nerves as we all try to move past the firefight and explosions from earlier. For a while, we focus on the food, as if savoring each bite might somehow keep the outside world at bay.

It's Moshe who breaks the silence. "Khalid, where were you during the fight this morning?"

Khalid's eyes flick over to mine for help, and I jump in before things get awkward. "I gave Khalid my gun and asked him to protect the children." My words hang there like a peace offering, hoping Moshe will take it and move on.

Moshe nods slowly, but I can tell the moment needs a bit of steering. A Bedouin's pride has been attacked.

"So, is everyone still okay with heading into Jordan?" I ask, hoping to shift the focus onto something more pressing than who was or wasn't where in the middle of the firefight.

Gabriel answers first, "Considering the bigger picture, I'm still in. Has anyone heard anything new about the armies around Israel?" His voice is calm, but the question reinforces the constant alarm we all feel.

"Nothing new," I reply. "Ariela mentioned the situation earlier, but no one's heard anything else since." I glance around the table, and everyone shakes their heads in agreement, signaling we're still operating on limited info.

As the conversation drifts back to practical matters, Khalid pipes up, "We have the basics for living, but it wouldn't hurt to have more food supplies. Who knows how long we'll be out there."

"And where exactly did Ariela go?" Khalid adds, clearly uneasy.

"She's off getting more information about the war," I say, dodging the question's more profound implications. "And maybe some supplies. She has... contacts in Eilat."

Devorah, ever perceptive, jumps in with a smile. "Thomas, Ariela seems like quite the catch. You're lucky to have her. Are you two married yet?"

I can feel the heat rising in my face. "Uh, well, we've been... discussing it," I mumble. Technically true. Sort of. At least in the last hour.

Moshe, ever the sage, chimes in, "Ah, Proverbs says, 'He who finds a wife finds a good thing.'"

"Thank you, Moshe." I wish the conversation would take a different direction, but Tabitha, clearly excited, isn't done yet.

"If we go into the desert for a long time, how will you get married? I mean, weddings require planning!" She looks genuinely concerned as if the organization of a wedding in the wilderness is more daunting than the impending war.

"I hadn't exactly thought that far ahead," I admit, feeling the topic shift unexpectedly.

Devorah's eyes light up like she's just found her new project. "Well, good news! Moshe is a rabbi. He can perform the ceremony!"

Hala, Khalid's wife, gives a knowing nod. "Ariela is Jewish. Are you... a goy?" She asks as if this minor detail could make or break the whole operation.

"Yes, I am a *goy*," I say, half-laughing. "But I don't think that's a problem, is it?"

Tabitha jumps in with all the enthusiasm of someone who's about to break some terrible news. "Under Israeli law, yes! Jews can't marry goyim in Israel. You'll have to go abroad to make it official."

"Well, that's... inconvenient," I mutter.

Devorah, ever practical, waves a dismissive hand. "Oh, don't worry about that. Moshe can perform the marriage once we're in Jordan!"

Rana, Salem's wife, perks up with a smile, sensing the chance to get involved. "But to respect Ariela's traditions, it must be a proper Jewish wedding. We'll need a yarmulke for Thomas, a chuppah for the ceremony, and, of course, a glass for him to break with his foot!"

"Oh, and a ketubah," Devorah adds eagerly. "A marriage contract outlining all of Thomas' obligations as a husband. Don't worry, Moshe can draw that up too."

Before I can respond, Tabitha claps her hands together like this is the best news she's heard all week. "And food! We need to think about food. There's challah bread, and don't forget the dancing!"

"And the parents," Hala says thoughtfully. "It's traditional for the parents to be there, right?"

The mention of parents causes a brief pang in my chest. "Uh, well, my parents passed away. It's just me."

Tabitha offers a sympathetic nod, "I'm so sorry. And what about Ariela's parents?"

"Her father is a widower, and with everything going on, it's not safe for him to travel," I say, knowing full well that Ariela's family is a complicated matter I can't delve into.

There's a brief silence before Devorah, ever the optimist, brightens. "No worries! We'll make this wedding a real event, and we'll be your family. Right, everyone?"

The group erupts in nods and excited chatter, the women practically tripping over each other to suggest ways to make this desert wedding happen. Even Gabriel and Moshe seem amused at how quickly this has spiraled into full-blown event planning.

"Maybe we can get a camel for you to ride into the ceremony!" Tabitha says, giggling.

"And we'll find someone to play music," Hala adds. "Perhaps a flute? A wedding needs music."

I sit there, bewildered but somehow charmed by how enthusiastic everyone is about the idea of a wedding—my wedding—in the middle of a desert, no less. I guess when life throws you into the apocalypse, you might as well plan a party.

To rein things in, I finally suggest, "Thank you all for your ideas. But let's... maybe discuss this with Ariela first?"

The group laughs, and Tabitha winks at me, "You better! She might have some opinions!"

As the conversation finally shifts back to survival tactics in the desert, my phone rings. It's Ariela from Eilat calling us to meet her at the warehouse.

I pay the bill—thankfully using the cash we "acquired" from those Quds Force terrorists—and we pile into our vehicles. The camaraderie from the restaurant follows us as we drive off, and I can't help but smile at the absurdity of it all. I left this morning as a single man, fought off terrorists, and by afternoon, I'm halfway to planning a wedding.

In the middle of a war zone. In the desert. With a group of well-meaning fellow travelers.

What could possibly go wrong?

Chapter 35

When you're single, you believe you have all the freedom in the world. No obligations, no compromises. But when that so-called "freedom" starts to get squeezed, it's... unsettling. The unexpected phone conversation with Ariela had already thrown me for a loop, but now? Am I ready to commit to someone? Especially with the world on the brink of chaos? I might need flexibility in the coming weeks—if we even have that long. And yet, here I am, driving into the unknown, a part of me considering marriage while the other part is preparing for war.

Oh, and the wedding talk. Let's not forget that. These women could hardly keep quiet about it! It was like a bridal magazine exploded in the middle of a military operation. But I get it. They'd just lived through a nightmare this morning, and planning a wedding was their way of finding some normalcy, or maybe just a distraction.

But am I ready to add "husband" to my list of responsibilities, alongside "survivalist" and "enemy of terrorists"? Ariela had said something earlier that hit me hard. Time is running out. In our situation, everything is compressed. What would usually take months—courting, engagement, marriage—now feels like it needs to happen in the span of a week, maybe less. Life is speeding up, and we're running out of time.

As we drive toward Eilat, I take the winding road that loops around the north of the city, then merge onto Highway 90, heading north. The convoy follows closely behind me, everyone keeping tight formation this time. We pass through the industrial zone and circle around a nondescript building, coming to a stop by the back gate.

A guard in plain clothes, holding an automatic rifle, opens the gate wordlessly and gestures for us to pull up to the gas pump. One by one, another man fills our vehicles with gas. Apparently, Ariela has enough pull with Shin Bet—or whoever these people are—to get us topped off like this. Benefits of being connected, I guess.

When our tanks are full, we are directed to move our vehicles and park at the far side of the lot. Khalid, Saleh, Moshe, and Gabriel get out of their vehicles and approach me. Khalid looks around warily, his eyes narrowing. "What is this place?"

"Some kind of warehouse," I answer. "Might be connected to the airport down the road."

Just then, an Israeli fighter jet roars overhead, shaking the ground beneath us. We all flinch at the sudden noise, a stark reminder that the quiet we've had for the past few days was temporary. There's a storm brewing, and it's not far off.

Gabriel rubs the back of his neck. "Where's Ariela?"

"Inside, I think. We were told to wait."

Everyone looks restless. We're only minutes away from the Jordanian border, yet here we are, lingering in some parking lot. After a tense few moments, Ariela finally emerges from the building, waving us over as two men roll out pallets stacked with boxes. She motions for us to pull our cars closer.

"Take these," she commands, pointing at the boxes.

Everyone gets to work, stuffing the vehicles with as many supplies as they can hold. The boxes are packed with food, medical supplies, and—of course—ammunition. I unload some of the older rifles and guns from my SUV. There are too many, and they take up too much space in my car. It's a reminder of the death I witnessed when in the desert.

When we're finished, she sends everyone back to the cars, except for me.

Arelia walks over, and she looks serious. "We don't have much time. I spoke to my superiors about what happened this morning, and they're analyzing the identity cards we found—especially the collaborator's. Things are... complicated. They've ordered me to keep a low profile."

"What's the status of the war?" I ask, cutting to the chase.

She pauses as if considering how much to tell me. "First, you need to know the collaborators have circulated my photo. The traitors working with Quds Force. My commander ordered that I must leave with you for Jordan and then... disappear."

Disappearing doesn't precisely sound comforting, but there's no time to dwell on that. "And the war? What's happening?" I press again.

"Nothing's certain yet, but there's a massive buildup of enemy forces. A coordinated attack is expected. Troops from the east are moving toward Syria, and more are being added to the south every day. The Israeli battle plan is, of course, classified, but trust me—our forces are ready. Our country has never been more united. But we need to go. Now."

"I wish we could ride together," I say, wanting more time to talk.

"I do, too," she replies, glancing at the fully loaded vehicles. "But we need drivers, and we can't waste any time."

Without another word, Ariela climbs into my SUV and waves for the rest of the convoy to follow her. As we pull out of the warehouse and head toward the Jordanian border, my mind races. I left this morning as a single man, but now? I've been thrust into a whirlwind of plans, war strategies, and a potential wedding. I glance at Ariela through the rearview mirror. Do I really have a choice? She's everything I've ever wanted—strong, decisive, and full of life. But is this the time to commit to forever when forever feels so ambiguous?

The border comes into view. Surprisingly, it's not jammed with cars, though there's a steady line of vehicles with Israeli plates heading into Jordan. Clearly, we're not the only ones who've decided to flee to the ancient land of Edom.

We inch forward, and the Israeli guards wave us through without much fuss. The Jordanian border guards do the same, and just like that, we're in Aqaba.

We stop briefly at a money exchange shop to trade our Israeli shekels for Jordanian dinars. The shop owner is quick, efficient, and doesn't ask any questions, which I'm grateful for. We've got more significant problems than currency conversions right now.

Back on the road, we head north, passing a sign for Petra and Wadi Musa. But our destination lies further east, in the wilderness of Edom. As I drive, I wonder what the others are thinking. We've left the familiarity of Israel behind and entered a foreign land. Are they as uneasy as I am?

Just then, my phone rings and I glance down at the screen. It's an unknown number. "Hello?" I answer, already bracing myself.

"Hello. This is Ariela's father," says a deep voice on the other end. "May I ask if you have a moment to talk?"

I nearly choke. "Yes, sir. I'm pleased to make your acquaintance," I reply, trying not to sound like a complete idiot. What do you even say to the Prime Minister of Israel—especially when he doesn't bother introducing himself formally?

Chapter 36

Hearing that voice on the phone sends a shiver down my spine. This isn't just any voice—it's a voice that commands armies. As I grip the steering wheel a little tighter, I brace myself. This conversation must be handled exactly right.

"I've spoken with Ariela," the Prime Minister begins, his words carrying authority, "and she's informed me of her desire to marry you."

Straight to the point. Not one for small talk. "It's all moving fast," I say, trying to sound composed.

"Frankly, I think it's reckless," he counters without hesitation.

That's a blunt assessment. At least he's honest. "It may appear that way," I reply cautiously.

"Are you committed to this?" He is not letting me off the hook.

"We've only known each other for a few days," I explain, "and while it wasn't exactly love at first sight, we've been through... extraordinary circumstances together. Did she tell you what happened?"

"Yes," he says, and for a moment, his tone softens. "I appreciate what you did for her—rescuing her from those terrorists. You've done a great deal."

"She's special, unlike anyone I've ever met."

There's a pause, then he chuckles. The Prime Minister, chuckling? "Believe me, I know she's unique. Stubborn as a mule, but with a heart of gold," he says with what I can only describe as paternal pride. "But listen," his tone turns serious again, "with everything going on, I want her safe. Can you promise me that?"

"To the best of my ability," I reply, knowing that's all I can give, but it's the truth.

"So, what's your decision?" His question feels like the final push. This isn't a casual chat.

"Sir," I begin, my voice steady, "may I ask for your daughter's hand in marriage?"

There's a short laugh on the other end, and I'm momentarily thrown. "I probably don't have much say in this," he says, almost amused. "Ariela knows her mind better than anyone, but... you have my blessing. Maybe this time it'll turn out better."

Wait. What does he mean by that? I blink, trying to process what he just said. "Thank you, sir. I'll do my best. But what did you mean by 'better this time'?"

He doesn't hesitate. "Didn't she tell you?"

"No..." I respond, feeling an uncomfortable twist in my gut.

"Ariela was married once before, right after her time in the IDF," he says, his voice more somber. "It lasted six months. The guy was a scoundrel, a disaster. He hurt her deeply. Don't be that guy."

Shock hits me like a punch to the chest. She was married before? Ariela never mentioned it. Not once. "I won't," I say firmly, though my mind is spinning.

"Good. Then I suppose we're moving forward."

"That's what we both want," I assure him, though my mind is still scrambling to process this new information.

"Alright, here's the plan," he continues, all business again. "When you reach the town of Mraigha, you'll find a Country Government Office. There, a marriage certificate will be waiting for you. It's seventy-five kilometers from your current position, one hour and two minutes away. After that, get Moshe Cohen, who's with you, to perform a proper Jewish wedding."

My head spins. "Wait—how did you manage that? And... how do you know our position and who's in our group?"

He doesn't miss a beat. "I work for the Israeli government. We have our ways. I can't stay on the line much longer. But before I go—" his tone softens slightly, "I wish I could be there. Maybe someday we'll meet in person."

"I hope so, sir," I say, my voice genuine. This conversation, despite its whirlwind of revelations, leaves me with an odd sense of connection to the man.

"*Mazel tov*," he says, and then the line goes dead.

I lower the phone, staring out at the Jordanian highway as the new truck—once owned by terrorists—glides smoothly over the asphalt. But my thoughts are anything but smooth. This day has been one giant roller coaster from the moment it started. First, a gun battle. Then a marriage proposal with Ariela. Wedding plans with the women thrown in like we're organizing a picnic. A stop at a secretive warehouse for supplies. An Israeli fighter jet buzzing us as a reminder that the world is on fire. And now, a conversation with the Prime Minister of Israel, who has apparently orchestrated our marriage certificate.

Oh, and the tiny detail that Ariela was married before. That's a big one. I'll need to wrap my head around it—sooner rather than later.

I glance ahead at my SUV, knowing Ariela is focused on the road ahead. She didn't say anything about her past marriage, and now I'm wondering why. Did she think it didn't matter? Or is it just something she doesn't want to revisit?

As we drive toward our unknown future, one thing's for sure: I've never had a day like this.

Chapter 37

I passed Ariana in my truck and now lead the convoy.

The road from Aqaba to Mraigha is a relatively straight run of just over an hour. The terrain consists of brown, barren hills on both sides, carved by centuries of wind and erosion. It's a stark, almost otherworldly landscape, and yet it feels ancient, as if the earth here holds secrets from millennia past.

There are few cars on the road, and most of them head north, like us. The small towns and settlements we pass seem modest, their low-rise, flat-roofed buildings blending into the sandy-brown surroundings. Life here is a testament to resilience.

Minarets rise above the towns, slender-like fingers reaching toward the sky. There's a sense of calm and resilience in the people who have learned to survive in this harsh environment. I wonder, though, how many here are aware of the chaos gathering around us—the armies poised for action, the world teetering on the edge of something far worse.

My thoughts return to our small convoy. Each person here carries their own uncertainties and questions about what lies ahead. This is an eclectic group of individuals with divergent backgrounds and beliefs and leading them into an unknown future is a heavy obligation. The enormity of it gnaws at me. Can we, with everything happening around us, really find common ground?

I glance at the side mirrors and catch sight of Ariana driving behind me. Our relationship looms large in my mind. My first marriage with Debbie ended in failure—am I setting myself up to make the same mistakes again, blinded by the urgency of the moment? Ariana and I have shared extraordinary experiences, but we come from such different worlds. Can an Israeli Jew and a gentile from a different culture genuinely make a life together?

The question feels too big and complicated for a quick answer. And maybe it doesn't even matter. Time is short, the world is unraveling, and perhaps all that truly matters is here and now. I'll have to place my trust in something larger than myself.

As I drive, I consider my core beliefs. For the first time in a long while, I feel God's presence keenly. I've always known He is there, but I've often kept Him at a distance. Now, though, I sense

His hand at work, not only in the military developments swirling around us but in His protective presence in my own life. Verses of assurance flood my mind: *"I will never leave you or forsake you. I know the plans I have for you, plans to give you a future and hope."* My faith feels stronger and more grounded., and I know that because of what Jesus did, I am a child of God.

Ahead, Mraigha comes into view, a small town nestled in the desert expanse. It's familiar from past archaeological expeditions. Navigating through the narrow streets, one senses that the population is wary of the events taking place not far from here. It's a quiet place—shops, a few hotels, some scattered eateries. The administrative building looms ahead, the Jordanian flag draped across its facade, a reminder of where we are and the delicate balancing act we're navigating.

I pull into a parking spot, and my group follows. We exit our vehicles, stretching after the drive. Ariela approaches me, curiosity in her eyes. "Why are we here?" she asks.

"I need to take care of some paperwork inside," I say, keeping things vague. "Want to come with me?"

The others gather around, their eyes filled with anticipation. Khalid, ever the pragmatist, asks, "What's the latest on the war?"

I nod toward Ariela. "Would you mind filling them in?"

"Of course," she replies, recounting the intelligence she received about the armies massing around Israel.

Moshe steps forward, his voice laced with curiosity. "And what about the supplies we picked up in Eilat? How did you manage that?"

Ariela's expression remains composed. "It's a warehouse that stores supplies for the IDF, the airport, and the town. I have contacts who are eager to help in these times. They made the offer, and I accepted."

The group seems satisfied with her explanation, nodding in quiet agreement.

I ask the group, "Can you wait here?" And to Ariela. "Come with me."

Inside the government office, it's like the town. Few people. The atmosphere is orderly, the air thick with the scent of paperwork and ink. I approach a glass window and, speaking in

Arabic, announce, "My name is Dr. Thomas Thornton. I was told to pick up some documents."

The clerk behind the window checks a registry and offers me a smile. "Please follow me to Mrs. Nadia Al-Mansoor's office."

He leads us down a corridor and knocks on a door. A woman's voice invites us in.

Nadia Al-Mansoor is poised, professional, and exudes authority. Her warm smile puts us at ease, her dark eyes sharp with intelligence behind her glasses. She welcomes us and immediately produces a couple of sheets of paper from her desk. "Dr. Thornton, we received your documentation from Amman. Is this your bride?"

I glance at Ariela. "Yes, this is her." I'm not entirely sure what documentation is required, but I go along with it, trusting the process.

Nadia continues, "You'll both need to sign the Marriage Contract and Certificate to make it official. I see it's registered as a Christian marriage. In Jordan, only Muslim and Christian marriages are recognized."

Her statement catches me off guard, but I don't let it show. Clearly, the Israeli Prime Minister had maneuvered this somehow, whether through political channels or some more discreet method.

"Do you have two witnesses to sign as well?" she asks.

I turn to Ariela. "Have you decided?"

"Decided?" She is caught off guard, not fully knowing what's going on. Then, she catches on. "We'll get them from outside," Ariela replies smoothly.

Nadia nods, allowing us to retrieve our witnesses. As we step outside, Ariela looks at me, a mixture of surprise and curiosity in her eyes. "What's really going on here?"

"You proposed marriage this morning, and I figured we might as well make it official," I say, meeting her gaze. "If you're having second thoughts, now's the time to tell me."

Ariela is momentarily speechless, her eyes widening. But then she laughs, shaking her head. "Unbelievable. Yes, let's do this."

We select Devorah the wife of Moshe, and Gabriel as our witnesses—Devorah because she's Jewish and close to Ariela, and

Gabriel because he fits the legal requirements for a Christian marriage. We instruct them to keep things simple and follow us inside.

Back in Nadia's office, she begins reading the Marriage Contract aloud, her voice formal and steady. "This Marriage Contract is entered into in accordance with Jordanian law, witnessed by two individuals." The contract outlines obligations—financial support, kindness, fairness. It's more detailed than I expected, but I listen carefully, nodding when Nadia asks for my agreement.

"I accept," I say, looking at Ariela as I pledge to support and care for her.

Ariela smiles, her eyes meeting mine. Nadia continues, reading the wife's obligations, that she is there to serve and obey her husband, and Ariela agrees just as firmly. Though I wonder silently about the "obedience" clause, this isn't the time for deeper discussions.

We sign the documents, Arabic script flowing from right to left across the page, and our witnesses do the same. Nadia gives us a final blessing and wishes us a happy union.

As we step outside, Devorah can barely contain her excitement. "Now we can have the real wedding before God—and a party!" she announces.

Ariela looks at her, baffled. "Party? What party?"

Devorah grins. "It's all been arranged."

Ariela shakes her head in disbelief. "Unbelievable."

Before I can even process everything that's happened, my phone rings. I answer, "This is Thomas Thornton."

A female voice speaking in Hebrew informs me that all the essentials for our wedding and celebration have been arranged at a nearby shop, and accommodations have been secured at a camp fifteen kilometers outside town. Everything has been paid for.

The efficiency of the Israeli government is staggering, even amid facing its biggest challenge ever. I hang up, marveling at how swiftly and seamlessly they've orchestrated everything.

As we get back in the truck, I can't help but wonder just how closely the Israelis are watching us. But there's no time to dwell on that.

Chapter 38

The day has been a whirlwind, beginning in the secret cave near Eilat and now, hours later, driving out of the quiet town of Mraigha in Jordan. Boxes from a local shop sit beside me on the truck's passenger seat, ordered by a mysterious liaison within the Israeli government—more precisely, someone working for the Prime Minister of Israel.

We drive westward, the desert stretching around us, until we spot a small sign for "Seven Pillars of Wisdom Bedouin Camp." Tucked away in a secluded valley, the camp is a luxurious haven, its colorful tents a welcome retreat against the desert's merciless expanse. Palms and vivid greenery hint at an underground reservoir.

As we approach, the camp's elegance is unmistakable. At the entrance, we're welcomed by a small group—four men and three women, all dressed in traditional Bedouin attire. Their eyes linger a moment too long on Khalib and Saleh, but Khalib's warm greeting dissolves any suspicions. A sense of relief and gratitude washes over our group.

"Thank you for the welcome. We have a reservation," I say in Arabic.

"Yes, the Dr. Thomas Thornton group," one of the men replies with a polite nod. "Two nights, correct?"

I hadn't expected two full nights here. In this oasis? It's more than we could have hoped for. "That's right. Is there a secure place for our vehicles?"

"They're safe where they are; they'll be guarded around the clock."

Once we're settled, I open the boxes we'd collected in Mraigha. Inside are ceremonial clothes: a flowing dress for Ariela, a crisp white shirt for me, and other items for Moshe to officiate. I distribute these items and then head for my tent.

My tent is reserved for executives, and it is the place where Ariela and I will spend out first night together as a married couple. Entering, I pause, absorbing the spacious interior. The blend of traditional Bedouin charm and understated luxury is perfect. A large bed draped in a soft duvet and layered with pillows stands waiting, and a faint perfume of cedar and spices lingers in the air. The elegance is intimate, private, and just for us—a setting made even more special by the thought of Ariela sharing it with me.

After a quick shower, I let the warm water wash away the tension of the day, and as I shave and change into clean jeans and the white shirt, my thoughts drift to Ariela. It feels surreal to consider the way our relationship has transformed. I remember the day I met her—a fierce, enigmatic figure with her rifle aimed directly at me. Now, that initial tautness has melted into something deeper, more intense than survival. Somewhere along the way, during chaos, I fell in love with her.

In my pocket, I carry a delicately carved gold ring, which I retrieved from my box of coins and jewelry. It was my mother's ring. Under the desert stars, we'll pledge our commitment in a traditional Jewish ceremony—a testament to the resilience of love.

Walking along a path, I arrive at the large dome tent where the wedding ceremony is to take place, and upon entering it, I stop in my tracks, captivated by the sight before me. Ariela stands there, draped in a beautiful Bedouin gown that hugs her figure, her dark hair spilling down her back like a waterfall. Until now, except for morning awakenings, I've only seen her with a ponytail. The gown's colors seem to echo the earth and sky, and her eyes—those intelligent, piercing eyes.

Every step brings me closer to her, my heart racing with each one. Her smile is radiant, filled with a blend of joy and calm that reaches across the space between us. I reach out, gently brushing a strand of hair from her face, then take the delicate veil from Devorah and carefully place it over Ariela's head. This simple act feels charged with tradition and meaning—a gesture of love and respect that holds centuries of symbolism. Through the veil's fabric, I meet her gaze and whisper a quiet prayer, asking for God's protection over her, over us, and for guidance as we step into the unknown life awaiting us. Our fingers meet, warm and steady, and I feel the same magnetic pull that has always drawn me to her.

Side by side, we walk toward the chuppah, a white canopy held aloft by Khalib, Saleh, Gabriel, and Shadi. This canopy, open on all sides, symbolizes the home we may never have in one place, a future filled with the unknown, but at this moment, all that matters is Ariela and me. Underneath, Moshe, our rabbi, smiles at us and begins the ceremony, his voice low and steady in the warm desert air.

Moshe lifts Ariela's veil, revealing her face—radiant, beautiful, and so close that I can see the emotions flickering in her eyes. He begins the *Birkat Erusin*, the betrothal blessing, reciting the ancient words over a cup of wine. As he hands it to us, Ariela's eyes meet mine as we drink, each sip filled with the hope of our promises.

I take her hand, slipping the simple gold ring onto her finger. Her smile broadens a pure, unguarded joy that touches me deeply. We exchange our vows, our words intertwining like threads in a tapestry of trust, commitment, and love that feels more profound than anything I've ever known. I am suddenly struck by the gravity and beauty of this bond—one that's grown from survival and forged in something unbreakable.

Moshe unfolds the *ketubah*, our marriage contract, and reads it aloud, outlining the promises we've made to each other. It was the exact text Nadia had read earlier in the day. He hands it to Ariela, who accepts it with a solemn nod, then invites us to share another sip of wine as he begins the *Sheva Brachot*, the seven blessings that evoke love, friendship, and the blessings of family and joy.

As Moshe finishes, he holds out a cloth-wrapped glass, and I take it, aware of the moment's importance. The glass in my hand is fragile, a reminder of the temple destroyed in Jerusalem, of sorrow that exists even in the most joyful times, and of the care required to nurture what Ariela and I have found. I place it on the floor, and with a single, swift motion, I bring my foot down, shattering it underfoot.

The guests erupt in a cheer of *Mazal Tov!* The words fill the air around us, and I look at Ariela, seeing the relief and happiness shining in her eyes. We're married.

As the guests disperse outside the tent, they leave us for a few moments alone inside. I take a place beside her, and for a moment, we sit in the quiet, letting the depth of this moment wrap around us like a warm blanket. I turn, feeling my heart brim with gratitude and love. "You're beautiful," I murmur, my voice heavy with emotion.

She smiles, a soft, knowing look in her eyes that sends my heart racing. "And you're handsome," she replies, reaching for my hand.

Our fingers intertwine, and in the stillness, I feel the enormity of the promise we've made. We sit side by side, bound together by a love that came unexpectedly as we survived every trial.

"I never imagined we'd end up here," I say, brushing my fingers across hers.

"Neither did I," she replies, her voice soft. "But it feels right."

I nod, and as if following an unspoken urge, I lean in and kiss her. It's not rushed or intense but slow, deliberate, and filled with the anticipation that lies ahead. Our lips meet, lingering in the quiet of the desert night.

When we pull back, her gaze is soft, her face radiant with happiness. "Let's join the others," she suggests, though her hand remains in mine.

We step out into the cool night, stars scattered above. Around the fire pit, our friends laugh and share stories.

As the night deepens, I take her hand and quietly lead her away. In silence, we walk, the vast desert stretching out in all its ageless beauty, the breeze playing with her hair as we make our way back to the quiet sanctuary of our tent.

Inside, the world fades until it's just the two of us. Ariela's gaze meets mine, and in her eyes, I see everything we've survived together—each battle, each fear, every lingering doubt. And yet, here we are, bound by something greater than either of us could have anticipated.

In the stillness of our first night as husband and wife, we hold each other close, our hearts beating in rhythm with the desert wind. And in that perfect intimacy, I know that no matter what dangers may lie ahead, we'll face them together—stronger, braver, and in love.

Chapter 39

The morning light filters gently into the tent, casting a soft glow on Ariela as she sleeps beside me. Her beauty, framed by the golden rays of dawn, takes my breath away. For a few moments, I watch her, amazed at the peace she exudes. The warmth between us, something more profound than mere affection, feels like it has been divinely orchestrated—a bond that words fail to capture. I want to reach out and touch her cheek, but instead, I let her rest.

Carefully, I slide out of bed, my movements slow so as not to disturb her. The words of Moshe echo in my mind, "He who finds a wife finds a good thing." The thought of her being more than a companion, being my partner in the deepest sense, stirs something inside me. A quiet longing that I didn't know was there.

The cold water from the shower jolts me fully awake, though not enough to erase the memories of last night—of her, of us. After dressing, I steal one last glance at Ariela before heading outside. The scent of desert herbs and freshly brewed coffee mixes with the morning air as I approach the others, all of them sitting under the canopy, awaiting whatever today holds. I know they think of Ariela and me, but no one says anything directly. Still, I catch the knowing smiles exchanged between Gabriel and Moshe.

"*Boker Tov*," I greet them, keeping my tone casual, though I feel their silent curiosity.

They respond in kind, Khalid and Saleh offering their Arabic version, "*Sabah al-kheir.*"

As we eat breakfast, there's an intense silence that hangs over the table, only broken by the occasional sound of utensils against plates. But Moshe, as expected, finally speaks up, breaking the spell.

"What's the latest on the armies?" he asks, his tone sharp with concern.

Khalid shares that Jordanian radio is filled with speculation, but there's no concrete news. Moshe, ever practical, turns to me. "Can Ariela check her short-wave radio for updates?"

"She will," I assure him.

Moshe pushes the topic further. "Does everyone still believe we're witnessing the end of days?"

Gabriel nods firmly, the conviction in his voice unwavering. "Yes. The signs are all there. The battle of Armageddon, the second coming of Christ—it's all in place."

Khalid chimes in, his tone equally resolute. "We Muslims believe Jesus will return, yes, but he will fight alongside the Mahdi to defeat the Dajjal. It's not just a Christian prophecy."

Moshe's expression tightens, his jaw clenched as he listens. "Jews believe the Messiah will come—yes—but not Jesus. It will be a descendant of David who restores Israel. And then comes peace."

"Jesus was a descend of David," Gabriel counters.

The conversation quickly heats up, the undercurrent of passion between them sharp as blades, though an air of civility masks it, at least for now. We have different beliefs, and each can be a source of conflict. Gabriel and Khalid speak with certainty, their faiths laying claim to the Messiah in very different ways, while Moshe's belief, too, remains steadfast.

"Who is this Mahdi?" I ask, curious, though I sense aggression rising.

Saleh, who has been quietly listening, jumps in. "The Mahdi will bring justice and establish the true faith," he says, with a finality that makes Moshe bristle.

"No, no," Moshe cuts in sharply. "There is no Mahdi. The Messiah is from David's line. That's the prophecy."

"You're missing the point," Gabriel adds, leaning forward. "The Messiah has already come. Jesus fulfilled the prophecy. It's all laid out in Matthew."

Moshe stiffens, the battle lines between them solidifying. "Jesus was a reformer, maybe even a prophet, but not the Messiah. His followers misunderstood him."

"He was more than that," Gabriel fires back.

Before I can intervene, Khalid raises his voice. "It doesn't matter what you believe. Non-Muslims will face judgment in hell unless they submit to Allah. This is the truth."

"And that," Moshe retorts, "is the problem with your religion. It's too black and white. It breeds conflict."

Gabriel doesn't miss a beat. "Satan distorts the truth. The Messiah doesn't need a Mahdi. Jesus is enough."

Their words carry a sense of finality. There is no middle ground. No room for negotiation. It's unsettling how easily this could unravel into something more dangerous. And yet, despite their passion, I know this isn't the moment for division. Not now.

At the same time, I need to give my position upon which my faith is based. Stepping into the silence, I ask a question that's been on my mind since this all began. "How do any of us expect to live up to God's perfection? Do we really think we can enter His presence on our own merit? If we are to die during this war, why should God accept us into his heaven?"

For a moment, no one speaks, my words settling in. I say, "I see the reason, the logic in what Jesus did, and why we need him. We would all agree that God is holy, and each of us is separated from him. We need some way to reconcile our fallenness with God's holiness, and God himself provided the solution."

Everyone waits as though expecting something more, so I continue. "It's not about performing rituals or doing good, for we can never achieve the level of perfection that God demands. For me, it's about grace. God loves every one of us and asks us to accept that He paid the price for our fallenness. Jesus did that. God asks us to accept that act as a free gift. Once we do that, we have faith in Him, and it means we don't have to do futile acts to gain God's favor, religious or otherwise. That means we have a daily relationship with God as our loving Heavenly Father. And yes, Jesus is coming again as the Messiah. At least, that's my belief." I hope I have not split the group because of what I said, but I had to make my beliefs clear.

Moshe stares at me, his brow furrowed, but before he can reply, the ground beneath us rumbles violently. Chairs and tables shake as the earth shakes with a force that leaves us clutching our seats. Devorah and Hala, just emerging from their tents, struggle to stay on their feet as the tremor passes.

Ariela then appears, walking down the path. "Is that the big one?" Ariela's voice draws my attention, and when our eyes meet, I feel a surge of warmth. Despite the chaos around us, she smiles, and for a moment, everything else fades.

"Not yet," I say, my voice steady though my heart still races from both the quake and her presence. "But it's coming."

As we regain our balance, I realize that the earthquake has done more than shake the ground. It's interrupted the mounting religious debate, perhaps even saved us from something worse. But the questions still linger, and as the rest of the group emerges from their tents, I know we're standing on the edge of something far greater than any of us can comprehend.

With a sigh, I turn to the group. "We need to figure out what's coming. Not just physically but spiritually. If we want to survive this, we need to understand the signs."

Gabriel nods in agreement, and the others look on. We've come this far together, but the question remains—can we stay united, even with the chasm of beliefs that divide us?

Chapter 40

After breakfast, the couples drift into their own worlds. Shadi, Hannah, and Layla play games among the palm trees, their laughter echoing against the rocky hills. At the same time, Ariela and I slip away to explore a trail leading into the hills, hoping to stretch our legs before the desert sun reaches its full ferocity.

It feels blissful to be alone together, and we walk hand in hand where the trail permits. Each step brings a warmth to my heart that I never expected to feel again. Ariela, my fierce and capable partner, reveals a softer side I never anticipated. A sabra, as they say, with her prickly exterior and sweet soul. I can't help but marvel at the bond we've formed amid the chaos surrounding us.

Our conversation flows easily, weaving between teasing flirtations and light-hearted anecdotes about our pasts. I find myself lost in her smile, momentarily forgetting the madness that looms over us. Yet, there's a nagging concern that needs to be addressed, and the golden light of the morning gives me the courage to lay my heart bare.

"This time," I begin, my voice trembling slightly with vulnerability, "I know I've found the right person. I hope you feel the same."

Her eyes lock onto mine, deep pools of contemplation. "What do you mean?" she asks.

"We've both made mistakes and had marriages that didn't work out," I confess, regretting the mention of past wounds. "But that shouldn't define us. It shouldn't define our relationship."

Ariela remains silent for a moment, her gaze unwavering. "We haven't really had the chance to talk about our lives," she replies softly. "How do you even know about my marriage?"

"It doesn't matter now," I say, hoping to redeem myself. "What's important is that I love you."

Her breath catches, the world around us fading into insignificance. "That horrid mistake was long ago," she murmurs, her voice thick with emotion. "I know you're different, Thomas. You have so many good qualities—kindness, strength, thoughtfulness. I want to be with you for the rest of my life, whatever that may entail."

Her words lifted a burden I didn't realize I was carrying. "And I feel the same," I reply, my voice catching with raw emotion. "I'm sorry for bringing up the past."

"No," she insists, her fingers brushing mine in a gentle acknowledgment of understanding. "It's okay. It needed to come out."

At that moment, I pull her close, wrapping my arms around her. We stand there, hearts intertwined, prepared to face whatever trials lay ahead.

After a few minutes, I shift the conversation, telling her about the religious debate that unfolded within our group earlier. "Do you think I should be concerned?" I ask, my unease clear.

Ariela considers my question carefully. "When beliefs lead to intolerance, that's when you should worry," she replies. "But it's also healthy for everyone to express themselves."

I nod, grateful for her perspective. "I hope these discussions won't escalate. Differences in beliefs can strain relationships, even among friends and couples."

"Passion can be constructive if channeled properly," Ariela says, placing a reassuring hand on my arm. "People fear what they don't understand. Open dialogue can help dispel misconceptions."

Encouraged by her words, I venture into deeper waters. "I've always been curious about your beliefs as a secular Israeli Jew. We've never really had the chance to discuss it, which feels important—especially before marriage. But it seems our courtship has been anything but traditional." I chuckle softly.

Ariela's eyes shine with openness. "I was raised in a secular Jewish household. My connection to Judaism is more cultural than religious. We're Zionists, and while I believe in God, I feel he's far away. I don't hold strong religious beliefs, but I respect those who do, and sometimes I am jealous of them. I have a longing for God."

I appreciate her honesty. "My faith as a Christian is significant in my life—or at least it should be. Before this war broke out, I was in a kind of dead zone. But now, with all that's happening, I find purpose and solace in my beliefs. I hope that won't become a point of contention."

Ariela looks thoughtful. "Many Israeli Jews feel uncomfortable around Christians, fearing they want to convert us. It feels like an intrusion, a disruption of our cultural identity," she explains, her voice heavy with history.

I understand the sensitivity of the topic. "I get that perspective. My philosophy is different. I believe in authentically living out my beliefs—albeit imperfectly. I engage in dialogue with those who want to discuss it. I trust God to work in people's hearts in His own time."

Ariela studies my face for sincerity. "So, you don't actively try to convert people?"

I shake my head gently. "No, I don't believe in forcing my beliefs on anyone. But I would like everyone to know God's love as found in Jesus."

She smiles, a hint of understanding crossing her features. "So, you're not one of those dogmatic missionaries we need to fear," she teases, her tone lightening the weight of the discussion.

I return her smile, grateful for her openness. "I hope not. The Apostle Paul, by the way, was a Jew. He proclaimed the good news of Jesus but reasoned with people without forcing them to believe."

Ariela furrows her brows, intrigued. "I find your perspective fascinating. It's true; many Jews harbor hostility toward Christianity due to our history of persecution. We fear that Christianity undermines Jewish rituals and beliefs," she admits.

I nod, fully aware of the scar's history has left. "Yes, the centuries of persecution have left deep marks. I grieve the atrocities committed by those who claimed to be Christians against Jews. Christians must recognize that God revealed Himself through the Jewish people, and we are woven into that narrative. To mistreat Jews is to disrespect God, at least in my belief."

Ariela raises an eyebrow. "As far as Jesus being the fulfillment of Judaism, I'm not sure I understand that."

I pause, searching for the right words. "What concerns me is that we may be in the end times. Moshe, Khalid, and Gabriel mentioned something important this morning: there will be judgment and a place of eternal punishment. I don't want anyone to go there. It's described as a place of torment. God has offered us a gift—a way out—by putting faith in Christ and believing in what He has done for us."

Ariela looks at me, her eyes filled with curiosity and contemplation. "It's a lot to take in, Thomas. I need time to think about this. I've never really considered your viewpoint."

I place a reassuring hand on her shoulder. "Take your time. These matters are complex, and everyone's journey with faith is unique. I'm here, and I want to understand your beliefs too."

We walk on in thoughtful silence, the air thick with unspoken questions. As we return to camp, I notice two military vehicles approaching from the other side, my heart racing at the sight. Could it be the Quds Force? Didn't we have enough trouble with them already? Why would they be here now?

Ariela and I left our handguns in the tent; we feel exposed. "Who are they?" I ask, a knot forming in my stomach.

"Let's go," she replies, her gentle demeanor morphing into the decisive military operative I know her to be.

We quicken our pace, urgency coursing through us as we draw closer to the camp.

Chapter 41

Panic pierces the air as we dash toward the camp. What if they're terrorists? Robbers? My heart races as the military vehicles rumble into the parking area. Ariela runs beside me.

"Any ideas?" I gasp, breathless from our sprint.

"Stay calm," she replies, her voice steady amidst the chaos. "Rushing in could provoke them."

We slow our pace. Men in military garb spill out of the vehicles, and a conversation unfolds between them and the camp manager. The words are lost to us, but the unease settles deeper in my gut. Then, they begin moving in our direction.

The camp manager comes beside me and in a low tone I ask, "What's their purpose?"

"Checking identities," the camp manager replies, his voice strained. "They come here from time to time."

I step forward, summoning every ounce of courage to mask my rising anxiety. "I am Dr. Thomas Thornton, the leader of this group."

The rest of our team emerges cautiously. The children gather around, eyes wide with apprehension, their innocence a stark contrast to what we feel.

A soldier steps forward, his gaze sweeping over us.

"We are verifying identities due to the influx of Israelis," he states, his tone clipped. "If you have vehicles with Israeli plates, we need to see your papers."

"Of course," I reply, steeling myself. "Everyone, get your identification cards and passports."

Wallets fumble open, ID cards retrieved. I grab my passport, anxiety spiking as I look at Ariela. She stands with her Israeli ID clutched tightly in her hand, the question of her military service looming ominously in the air.

"Why so many visits to Jordan?" the commander asks, examining my passport, its pages marked with countless Jordanian visa stamps.

"I'm an archaeologist," I explain, forcing calm into my voice. "I've collaborated with Jordanian antiquities organizations on various excavations."

The commander nods, returning my passport. Ariela steps forward, presenting her ID. I intercept the question before it can slip out, offering our marriage documents as a shield for her identity.

"We were just married," I say quickly. "She didn't have time for a name change." Ariela and I never discussed this, and it really doesn't matter.

The commander's interest piques at the mention of our marriage. "A Jordanian Christian contract," he observes, his eyes narrowing slightly.

"It is," I confirm, hoping to deflect any further scrutiny. Two married Christians provide a protective cover against any suspicion about Ariela's affiliation with Shin Bet.

Satisfied, the commander hands back the ID cards and my passport. "Where are you headed?"

"Into the desert," I reply, trying to maintain eye contact, though unease gnaws at my insides.

His gaze lingers on us, his silence charged with unspoken questions. "I wish you luck. These are serious times."

"Any news about the war?" I press, driven by a need to understand the threat hanging over us.

"The situation remains tense," he responds cryptically. "Large armies from the east have moved into Syria and Lebanon. We're vigilant, ensuring no external forces breach Jordanian borders, but Jordan is not their intent."

"Has a battle erupted?" I ask, desperation creeping into my voice.

"I'm not authorized to divulge much, but no major battles yet. The most troubling news is the financial crisis. Markets are crashing due to this situation, and people are in shock."

"Thank you for the update," I say, though my mind reels under the seriousness of what he shared.

The soldiers retreat to their vehicles. Once they're gone, Moshe's voice cuts through the silence, echoing our collective concern. "Can we get news on the shortwave radio?"

"Absolutely," Ariela says, her voice steady, a thin veil of calm over the chaos.

After lunch, the group gathers around a table, teacups in hand, a fragile semblance of normalcy in a world unraveling. Ariela tunes her shortwave radio, the crackling signal a lifeline to the outside chaos. The news washes over us, confirming the soldier's words—armies amassing, aggressions escalating, and a global financial crisis tightening its grip on the world.

Amid this turmoil, Ariela and I retreat to our tent, seeking solace in each other's arms. The luxury of a shower, once a mundane routine, now becomes a cherished memory as we prepare for the hardships ahead. On the bed, Ariela's eyes search mine, her voice laced with concern.

"What does your New Testament say about these times?" she asks, her brow furrowed.

"It speaks of upheaval and chaos," I reply, reaching for my worn Bible. "In Matthew 24, Jesus foretells false messiahs, wars, famines, and diseases. The fig tree budding, interpreted as the rebirth of Israel, indicates the nearing of his second coming."

"That's intriguing. What else?" Ariela inquires, her eyes reflecting curiosity but shadowed by fear.

"Many books of the New Testament address societal decay, moral confusion, and a turning away from God," I continue. "In Revelation, strange allegories describe future events: sores afflicting people, seas turning to blood, the Euphrates drying up, and earthquakes shaking the foundations. Yet, people curse God."

Ariela shudders, the reality of my words sinking in like lead. "It's terrifying. Some of these have happened."

"Yes," I confirm, sorrow heavy in my voice. "The armies from the east, crossing the Euphrates, fulfill a prophecy. In the following chapters, evil forces rise, leading to the final battle. These warnings echo those given by Ezekiel and Daniel but with greater detail."

She looks at me, her eyes pleading for reassurance. "What happens to those armies?"

"The Book of Revelation describes fire and brimstone raining down, reminiscent of Sodom's destruction," I explain. "I've visited Sodom's archaeological site; the evidence of intense fire is undeniable. The same fate awaits those attacking Israel. Their destruction will leave no doubt about the origin of this judgment."

"We live in a messed-up world," Ariela says, her voice a mixture of despair and resignation.

"But there is hope," I assert, meeting her gaze, desperation igniting my resolve. "Jesus, the Messiah, said he will return, and it's likely to be soon. It will be an unbelievable moment."

She takes a moment to absorb my words, her brow furrowing in contemplation. "Yes, that does bring hope. Is there anything I need to do?"

"Not much," I reply, my tone gentle yet resolute. "Just thank Jesus for what he has done for you, and then accept him, receive him, and then He gives the right to become his child. There are no rituals to perform."

Ariela hesitates, searching my face for sincerity. After a moment of deep reflection, she speaks, her voice steady. "Then I can do that, for I don't see how it interferes with my identity as a Jew. I see how it all fits together."

"It doesn't interfere," I affirm. "In fact, it perfectly fulfills who you are. As the Apostle Paul said, 'to the Jews first and then the Gentiles.'"

Ariela's eyes widen in realization. "Wow, that's a revelation. I never considered myself religious, but this... it's like an invisible heaviness on my soul has been taken away."

"That's called God's spirit," I explain. "And for sure, you are not religious. Religions are belief systems—attempts by humans to win God's favor through rituals or good actions."

"I now understand."

"It can take time to sink in."

"There's something else," she states, her voice trembling slightly. "Are we cowards for leaving Israel?"

"I've wondered that too. In the Book of Daniel, it's prophesied that the King of the North will invade the Beautiful Land," I reply, my heart heavy. "Much of modern-day Jordan will be safe. We're following Jesus's command to 'get out.' It's not cowardice; it's obedience to a divine order."

"But I feel guilty," she admits, her voice a fragile whisper.

"You, Esti Yitzhak, were ordered to leave," I remind her gently. "Your safety ensures your father's ability to lead and protect the nation. It's a strategic move, not cowardice."

Her confusion fades into understanding, and she meets my gaze. "How did you know about Esti Yitzhak?"

"Archaeologists have a way of uncovering truths," I say, forcing a smile.

Ariela takes a deep breath, gratitude radiating from her. "It must remain a secret."

"Absolutely," I assure her, the gravity of our situation hanging thick in the air. "Your safety is paramount."

She leans in, her lips brushing against mine in a soft kiss. "Thank you, Thomas."

"I love you, Ariela," I say, my words a promise against the storm brewing outside. "And no matter what, I hold you to the marriage contract, which I didn't write."

She laughs, a musical sound that feels fragile against the backdrop of chaos. "That document is a bit old-fashioned, isn't it?"

"A contract is a contract," I chuckle, though a shiver of dread races down my spine. "The expectations of the wife are clear; household affairs are overseen, and the rights and privacy of the husband are respected."

She playfully hits my shoulder, her eyes glinting with mischief. "We'll see about that."

Chapter 42

The following day, breakfast feels like a solemn ritual, the air thick with an unspoken unfriendliness. Despite the joy of being with Ariela last night, now, I am feeling the responsibility for our safety and survival. Our destination lies twenty-five kilometers east of the town of Ma'an, deep into the arid wilderness. For some unknown reason, the group puts their faith in me.

After loading the vehicles, I take the wheel of the truck, leading the convoy. Our first stop is Ma'an for fuel and fresh provisions before the final stretch of our journey. The ancient city, steeped in history, has seen the rise and fall of empires, from Romans to Byzantines and beyond. Its rich past is a treasure trove for archaeologists, and I can't shake the thought of the undiscovered relics hidden beneath the dust.

Water remains our most pressing concern. Jordan is one of the driest countries on earth, and I've chosen a specific location—Nabatean ruins, which I discovered years ago boasting a well that could sustain us. Petra's ancient marvels exemplify the incredible water systems that once thrived here, transformed into lush oases.

As we roll into Ma'an, my phone rings, jolting me from my thoughts.

"Hello," I answer.

"Thomas, this is Ariela's father," he says, his voice urgent.

"This is unexpected, sir."

"I don't have much time. I arranged for you to acquire three more Bedouin-style tents in Ma'an. Your two-person tent will be cramped for extended stays. From above, you'll look like a Bedouin camp."

His words send a shiver down my spine. Surveillance? I quickly jot down the address.

"How was the wedding?" he asks.

"Wonderful. Thank you for providing that." I reply. "Everyone appreciated the Bedouin tourist camp. I wanted to send you a video. Can you give me your email address?"

"Give the video to Ariela; she'll know where to send it."

His reticence is tangible, and as he hangs up, a cold knot forms in my stomach. His words linger ominously—will I ever hear from him again?

We arrive in Ma'an, and I direct our vehicles to the designated shop. After parking, I inform the group about picking up tents. The women venture into nearby shops while Khalid and Salem remain vigilant by the cars. Despite the apparent calm, Ma'an teeters on the edge of desperation in these war-torn days.

Inside the shop, I'm relieved to know Zevi Yitzhak has already covered the costs for the tents. After negotiating, I secure additional rugs, a large tarp for shade, and purchase a long rope and metal bucket for drawing water from the well. Ariela, using the shop's internet, sends her father the wedding video, her face a mask of concentration as she focuses on her task.

With the new tents piled high in the truck, the women return, their arms laden with fresh vegetables and large sacks of flour. We depart Ma'an, the modern road winding through the landscape that once hosted ancient trade routes linking Africa and Persia. I steer the convoy eastward onto a dirt road, avoiding unwanted attention from the nearby King Feisal military airbase.

As we drive deeper into the desert, remnants of ancient copper mines appear along the way, a testament to centuries of human endeavor. Here, where there are mines, there are towns, and I recall discovering one nearby a few years ago.

Leading our convoy further, I find the Nabatean ruins nestled between the hills. As we pull into the valley, I stop the truck.

"This is it," I declare, trying to infuse optimism into my voice.

Khalid surveys the area, his expression unreadable. "This is a good place," he says, but I sense his instincts are at work, measuring factors I can't comprehend.

While Khalid expresses his approval, fatigue weighs heavily on the others' faces. The shift from our previous comforts to this harsh landscape is evident.

Ariela looks around, her brow furrowing. "This place offers good defense against anyone coming up the road," she notes, her voice firm.

Prioritizing water, I make my way to the well, the lifeblood of our campsite. I had discovered this well long ago, its sturdy stone walls a testament to the ingenuity of the Nabateans. Dropping a tin bucket into the depths, the reassuring splash resonates like a distant promise—fresh, drinkable water. A small victory but a vital one.

Throughout the day, we set up our tents and establish our camp. Layla and Hannah tend to the goats, Shadi engineers a latrine, and Gabriel and Ariela inspect the camp's perimeter, strategizing our defenses.

As evening descends, we gather beneath the large tarp, the shadows of our circumstances lingering like a heavy fog. The atmosphere grows thicker, our conversation subdued, the reality of our situation pressing down on us.

Later, in the privacy of our tent, Ariela curls close to me.

"I wonder," she begins softly, "if you believe in miracles."

"What do you mean?" I ask, meeting her gaze.

"Isn't it a miracle that we are together?" she muses, her eyes reflecting a mixture of hope and fear.

A genuine smile breaks across my face. "The odds of us being here like this are astronomically slim. Divine intervention, obviously."

"I feel the same," she admits, her voice barely a whisper. "Are you happy?"

"For finding you, it's the greatest joy imaginable," I confess. "But I mourn for the chaos in the world."

She nods, a flicker of understanding passing between us. "There's not much we can do now except wait and see how this unfolds."

"But there is hope," I remind her, my voice steady.

"How so?" she presses, her brow furrowing.

"We read it before. In Ezekiel 39, it says the world will recognize God. That's something."

"It's too much to imagine," she whispers, her voice trailing off.

Before I can respond, Ariela's breathing evens out, signaling her descent into sleep.

I lie awake, fatigue pressing against me. I think back to our journey—from digging in Jerusalem's soil to navigating trials in the Negev, now finding solace in this vast expanse of desert with a remarkable woman by my side. I whisper a prayer of gratitude for our unlikely union, for the protection surrounding us, and for what lies ahead.

Chapter 43

The day begins slowly, the sun creeping over the horizon as, one by one, the members of our group emerge from their tents, their sleepy eyes clouded with confusion. Over the past few days, we have been driven by a singular purpose: escape the clutches of terrorists and robbers and seek safety. Now, we stand at a crossroads, enveloped by the harsh reality of our situation. This is our camp, our makeshift home, where we must weather the approaching storm.

Without the familiar routines of our past lives to anchor us, we feel adrift. What's for breakfast? Will we eat as a group or as families? Who will take charge of cooking? How do we ration our dwindling supplies? Do we need someone on guard to watch the trail? How much water lies in the well, and how quickly will it replenish? These questions swirl around us, both practical and existential.

Determined to instill some semblance of order, I set to work preparing a large pot of oatmeal with dates and chopped figs, a simple dish that has become my specialty. The campers seem grateful for the effort.

I brew coffee next, another of my talents, and when everyone gathers beneath the large tarp, I take a deep breath. "This is all new for us. Let's try to get organized, at least at a basic level. We can figure things out as we go along."

A lively discussion ensues, culminating in a collective agreement to share all meals as a group to conserve supplies and effort. That evening, we will gather again to discuss any tasks that need attention. Khalid and Salem will scout the area for resources, the kids will care for the goats, and Moshe and I will inspect the well and the ruins around it. Ariel and Gabriel will work out a plan of defense, finding the optimal places where we will take up positions, if necessary. The women will finish arranging supplies from our vehicles, and we will ensure we keep essential items close by in case we need to move quickly.

As the day wears on, each of us focuses on our assigned tasks. Evening falls, and Hala and Rana prepare a delicious Bedouin feast. We sit in a circle in our camp chairs, the flickering firelight casting shadows on our faces.

Moshe breaks the silence, asking the question that looms over us all. "Is there any news of the war?"

Ariela's expression darkens. "There's still a massive buildup. It's strange, isn't it? Nations mobilizing on such a scale. From a human perspective, it doesn't make sense."

Her words echo ominously in the stillness of the desert night. I glance at her, aware she likely has more information from an earlier satellite call with her father. I respond cautiously, "If we understand the prophecies correctly, this buildup takes time. Revelation speaks of *'demonic spirits going out to gather the kings of the world for the battle on the great day of God Almighty.'* Moving hundreds of thousands of troops isn't something that happens overnight."

Moshe adds gravely, "We must recognize that a spiritual battle is taking place, one far greater than any earthly conflict."

Gabriel nods, his expression serious. "God's forces will ultimately triumph over evil. The Beast and the False Prophet, along with all who follow them, will face judgment."

The gravity of his words weighs heavily on us. A thick silence envelops the group, the enormity of the spiritual conflict sinking in. Somehow, we are not just spectators; we are active participants in a cosmic struggle between light and darkness.

Ariela breaks the silence, her voice trembling slightly. "But why? Why must it come to this? What is the purpose behind all this suffering and destruction?"

I pause, allowing her question to settle in. "In the grand scheme, there's a purpose beyond our understanding. Perhaps it's about free will—the choices humanity makes. God allows us the freedom to choose our paths, even if some rebel against Him, embracing darkness. But in the end, light will triumph."

Gabriel adds, "It's a testament to God's justice. He is giving every soul a choice. Those who align with evil will face the consequences of their actions."

Ariela listens, her brow furrowed in thought. "It's hard to comprehend. The fall of the Beast, the battle of Armageddon... it feels surreal. Where do we fit into this divine plan?"

Moshe's gaze sharpens. "We play our roles by remaining faithful, standing firm in our beliefs, and clinging to hope, even when despair seems overwhelming. Every act of kindness, every display of love, reverberates in the spiritual realm. We may not see the full picture, but God does. Our purpose is to endure, to hold onto our faith, and to guide others."

I nod, wanting to respect his wisdom but feeling the need to emphasize another aspect. "There's more to consider—God's love. As a follower of Jesus, I believe we must accept His love, as shown by His sacrifice on the cross. We need to ponder how this love fits into our current situation."

"How does it fit into this chaos?" Ariela presses.

Taking a deep breath, I try to articulate the profound nature of God's love. "Throughout history, His love has been a guiding force. Even now, amidst the turmoil, His love remains. It's not solely about wrath and judgment; it's about redemption."

I gesture around us, the moonlight casting eerie shadows over the ruins. "In these end times, God's love manifests in various ways. It gives humanity a choice, a chance at redemption. Amidst the darkness, there are moments of grace. People are waking up and finding faith. Even now, in the face of impending destruction, God offers a path of repentance."

Hala, her voice soft yet powerful, adds, "In the stillness of the night, where stars fill the sky, God's love is evident. His love is the oasis in this barren land, a well that never runs dry. It's like a mother camel nurturing her young. God's love beckons us, guiding us forward, even when the path seems impossible. We understand how He came to us through Jesus. God is love, even in this frightening world."

Her words are surprising and linger in the air, blending with the night's stillness. How has this young, poetic Bedouin woman come to this understanding?

Ariela shifts uneasily. "But what about those who have chosen darkness? What about those who commit unspeakable acts?"

I acknowledge her question. "God's love extends to them, yet it respects free will. Those who choose evil separate themselves from that love. But His justice is intertwined with His love;

judgment is not an act of anger but a necessary step toward restoration."

Ariella's gaze remains fixed on the flickering campfire. "So, even amid the chaos, God's love is a guiding force. Can the world really experience His grace in its darkest hour?"

Silence falls over our circle as we absorb the implications of her question. The desert seems to hold its breath, the darkness pressing closer. As the night deepens, the air thickens with something profound, frightening, and otherworldly.

Suddenly, a distant sound cuts through the stillness—a low rumble, like thunder on the horizon. Instinctively, we all turn our heads toward the sound, hearts racing. The air feels charged with electricity, and the tension is obvious as we exchange worried glances.

"What was that?" Moshe asks, his voice barely above a whisper.

Khalid, who had been scanning the horizon, stands abruptly, his expression shifting from calm to concern. "I don't know, but we should be vigilant. We might not be alone out here."

The realization washes over us: we are camped in the open desert, exposed to threats both seen and unseen. A shiver runs down my spine, and I can feel Ariela's hand grip mine tightly, her earlier fears now mingling with a fresh wave of anxiety.

I glance around, the flickering flames of our fire casting erratic shadows across the ancient ruins, where countless lives have come and gone, and now we stand at a precipice of our own making.

"We need to keep watch," I declare, my voice steady despite the rising nervousness. "Let's break into shifts. Khalid, can you take the first watch? I'll take the second. The rest of you, try to get some sleep."

As we reorganize ourselves into a watchful guard, the world around us feels more dangerous than ever. The so-called End Times is a concept that is almost impossible to fathom, yet we are in it. As I look into Ariela's eyes, I know that the journey ahead will demand more than we've ever imagined.

We might be standing on the edge of something monumental, a battle not just for survival but for the very soul of humanity. The flame of hope flickers, and as we settle into the night, we brace ourselves for whatever may come, knowing that together, we must face the darkness ahead.

Chapter 44

For almost a month now, we have thrived in this forlorn landscape, where desolation has somehow transformed into a semblance of home. I often ponder the ancient Nabateans who once thrived here, mastering the copper mines not far from our camp. Even in a hostile environment, the human spirit can adapt and flourish.

Khalib and Saleh have become our guides, imparting wisdom on how to harmonize with this arid expanse. Their light, flowing garments shield them from the sun, and their vibrant culture bursts forth through poetry, music, dance, and the timeless art of storytelling. Hala and Rana have taught us to savor the delights of Bedouin cuisine, and their meals are a celebration of flavor that nourishes both body and spirit.

The well, a hidden treasure, has gifted us with a steady flow of water—an echo of the ingenuity of the Nabateans. The goats graze happily on the ample vegetation, and their rich milk has become a vital ingredient in our daily feasts.

Each week, we embark on a journey to Ma'an in my SUV and one of the trucks, a lifeline that grants us a much-needed respite from our rugged existence. The town's bustling market invites us to indulge in the flavors of beef, lamb, and chicken—luxuries we once took for granted. As we wander through the stalls, the aroma of spices dances in the air, reminding us of life's simple joys.

Yet, the landscape is not merely tranquil. Each day, fighter jets roar above us, their ominous presence hinting at the chaos unfolding beyond our sheltered existence. Jordanian Air Force planes zip through the sky, joined by an increasing number of foreign forces, and their collective might be a forerunner of the conflict escalating on the borders.

The war's shadow looms larger. The Israeli Iron Dome, while effective, stands as a lone guardian against a flood of enemy missiles. Reports from the north speak of overwhelming troop movements and foreign armies gathering just across the border in Syria, their numbers unfathomable. It takes time to mobilize that many troops.

Despite the encroaching darkness, our group clings to hope. During the past weeks, we have immersed ourselves in the prophecies of Ezekiel and Revelation, unraveling the divine tapestry of events that seem to mirror our present reality. While Moshe has given us insights into the Old Testament, Gabriel has expanded this with truths from the New Testament, especially about Jesus and the purpose of his coming. As the adage goes, there are no atheists in foxholes, and we find ourselves transformed by this shared understanding.

There seems to be a realization among members of the entire group that Jesus was more than a good man or prophet. His power over the physical world, his miracles, and his teaching are evidence that he is God who came as a man. He died so that we might live.

Evenings are spent huddled around the crackling shortwave radio, where grim news continues to unfold. Tonight, the announcer reveals that an immense force has broken through Israeli defenses and surged from Damascus, advancing into the Valley of Megiddo—an ancient crossroads steeped in prophecy.

As we listen, the chilling update brings us to the edge of despair. The enemy army from the south has pressed into the Kidron Valley, encroaching upon Jerusalem itself. Hand-to-hand combat erupts in the streets of the holy city.

Moshe's voice trembles with urgency, "This is terrible news." But as if to punctuate his words, the earth trembles beneath us— a ferocious quake that throws us from our chairs. The ground shakes as if the very fabric of reality is unraveling, and I scramble to steady myself, hands pressed against the earth, breathless with both fear and awe.

Ariela is beside me, her voice barely a whisper, "What do you think? Is that the big one?"

"It must be," I reply, heart racing.

The quake rumbles on, and when silence returns, we gather ourselves, shaken but intact. Devorah twisted her wrist in the chaos, and Ariela rushed to assist her. We crowd around the radio, relieved to find it still operational. The announcer, his voice strained, speaks of destruction on the coast north of Tel Aviv. What comes next?

In the hour that follows, we learn of devastation echoing across the globe. Cities tremble under nature's wrath, but this, I realize, is not merely an earthquake; it resonates with the prophetic words of Revelation.

"A great earthquake occurs as an angel pours out the seventh bowl," I murmur, realization dawning.

"Do you believe that was it?" Moshe asks.

Gabriel's voice is steady yet charged with anticipation, "It must be, but there's more. The next part speaks of great stones falling from the sky, and then fire will rain down, obliterating the armies that surround God's people."

"Is that where we find ourselves?" Moshe's eyes widen, a mix of optimism and dread.

Before Gabriel can respond, a low rumble reverberates through the air, a sound that thrums with ominous energy. We turn toward the west, and suddenly, the sky erupts in a cascade of radiant light, illuminating the darkness as if the heavens themselves have split open.

Far to the west, from the depths of the night, fire rains down, an inferno cascading toward the earth like a celestial judgment. We are transfixed, awed, and terrified, witnessing the annihilation of armies that once stood formidable. Their mighty war machines—symbols of power—now succumb to the divine onslaught, reduced to mere ash and ruin.

"The heavens weep fire upon the enemies," Rana breathes, her voice trembling with reverence.

In this moment, as flames dance across the horizon, our group instinctively draws closer together. Talya huddles beside Hala and Rana, while Khalid and Salem stand watchful and protective. Moshe stands firm, a steadfast presence as Devorah leans against him, this extraordinary moment pressing upon us all. I take Ariela in my arms, holding her tightly as we bear witness to this overwhelming spectacle.

Amidst the devastation, a flicker of understanding ignites within us. This is not merely destruction; it is the culmination of divine justice, a cosmic battle finally unveiled. The anguished cries of once-mighty armies echo in the distance, a testament to God's sovereignty.

Khalil sinks to his knees, tears streaming down his face. "There is no God like the God of our forefather Abraham. God gave His only Son so that we might not perish but have everlasting life." His revelation is profound, a moment of clarity amid chaos. "Father, forgive me, for I am a sinner," he cries out, and we join him in silent prayer, hearts heavy with humility and awe.

As the flames gradually subside, we lower our gaze to the ground, the remnants of destruction flickering in our memories. No words can capture the enormity of what we have witnessed.

"The fire has consumed them all," Moshe finally says, his voice thick with emotion. "Ezekiel states that from this day forward, the people of Israel will know that I am the Lord their God." Tears slip down his cheeks, and in agony, he confesses, "Oh God, too often I've treated You as an academic concept rather than the living God. Forgive me and forgive my rejection of the salvation You offer."

We remain silent, our hearts intertwined in a shared understanding of the magnitude of this moment.

Finally, Ariela asks, "What we have just witnessed is a miracle. But, Thomas, what comes next?"

"Many things, my love. The Messiah will return imminently. Just as He ascended, we will see Him come again. There will be a final judgment of evil, and those whose names are written in the Lamb's Book of Life will be saved."

Ariela's eyes shine with tears, and she asks, "And what of Jerusalem? Will it endure?"

"I once feared for the city's fate, but now I see clearly. This is not the end. It's not the last Jerusalem. It is the beginning. God has preserved Jerusalem. It will be transformed into a New Jerusalem, heralding a new heaven and a new earth. The details may be a mystery, but one truth stands firm: God's compassion for His people will not waver."

"Then we must believe," she whispers, a fragile yet resolute light glimmering in her eyes.

I turn to Moshe. "Perhaps you could lead us in a prayer of thanksgiving."

His voice is a gentle tremor as he lifts our spirits in a Hebrew prayer, gratitude pouring forth like a river.

We talk long into the night, our hearts overflowing with emotions too profound for words. Each of us feels a sacred connection to this moment, the ground we stand upon imbued with divine promise.

Later, as Ariela and I retreat to our tent, she asks, "Do you think my father made it?"

"I believe so. It is the foreign armies that have been consumed," I reply, hoping to comfort her.

She nods slowly, questions dancing in her eyes. "What's next for you and me?"

I smile gently. "Good question. I'm not entirely sure how the future unfolds, but I'm convinced that God has plans for us. We may not know how much an archeologist and a Shin Bet operative can contribute, but I trust He has significant tasks ahead for us. We will not worry. I am just thankful to have you with me."

As we lie together, Ariela drifts into a peaceful sleep while my mind races with wonder. I've spent my life piecing together the fragments of history, but now, clarity washes over me. History is not a series of random events; it is a journey leading to the fulfillment of God's magnificent plan. The Messiah will come, and we will stand before Him, the realization of God's eternal kingdom finally established.

In the tranquil embrace of the night, surrounded by the remnants of divine intervention, I find solace. A profound assurance settles within me, echoing the promise of a glorious future rooted in the boundless love of God. In this future, hope reigns eternal, and we are united under His everlasting grace.

A Conversation with the Author

How did you get the idea to write this book?

It started with a simple question. What would you do if you were in Jerusalem the day that the Battle of Armageddon started? The story unfolded from there.

It seems you left out many end times events. Why?

Yes, I purposely didn't include many things taking place before the return of Jesus Christ, such as the Rapture, the Tribulation, the bowls of judgment found in Revelation 16, the third temple, and so much more. I attempted to keep it simple by positioning the story between two major events. The first is found in the Book of Revelation, Chapter 16, where the armies of nations gather around Israel. Second, in Ezekiel 38:22, God will pour out torrents of rain, hailstones, fire, and sulfur on the armies attacking Israel. Those two events set the frame for Thomas and Ariela's adventure.

I'm sure some prophecy students will feel that something important has been neglected. The Last Jerusalem is not intended to be a theological exposition but rather a story of survival, love, and faith as the characters examine their beliefs. At the same time, I hope this book might cause readers to consider where history is going and the spiritual forces involved. Most importantly, I hope the story encourages readers to reflect on, accept, and rest in God's grace as given by Jesus Christ.

Did you have any issues with writing this book?

Honestly, it opened a Pandora's box of issues because I had to navigate my way through the complex world of Biblical prophecies and interpretations. One estimate is that up to 27% of the verses in the Bible deal with prophecy, and theologians have held different understandings throughout the centuries. Diving into this topic can be daunting but inspiring.

How much does your novel follow the chronology of events leading up to the Battle of Armageddon?

If you read Biblical prophecies, you will see that a lot is going on in the end times, and it is not always clear about the order of events or timing. For instance, how many days, weeks, or months will the buildup to the ultimate battle involve, and how long will the fight take place? Remember, we are talking about actual armies that need to be transported around the world.

Gog is mentioned in the book. What is Gog?

Some scholars treat Gog as symbolic, but many interpret it as a leader from Russia, and they have good reasons for doing so. My novel follows this interpretation. Others say it could be someone from Türkiye. What we know from Ezekiel is that God will judge Gog with pestilence and bloodshed for his persecution of God's people.

Are we in the last times?

I tend to believe so, but a few more critical things need to happen. In Ezekiel chapter 37, it speaks of the dispersion of the Jews. Then, they came back to their homeland as one nation, no longer split between Judea and Samaria. In Matthew 24, Jesus uses an illustration by saying that when you see the fig tree put out its leaves, then the end time is near. Many Biblical scholars see the fig tree as symbolic of the founding of the nation of Israel in 1948. In other parts of the Bible, there are descriptions of godless beliefs and perverse practices in society that emerge before the end times. There is a turning away from God and His truth. If you put all these prophecies together, the coming Day of the Lord is difficult to deny.

You briefly mentioned Babylon in the story. Who, what, or where is this Babylon that will be destroyed in the end times?

In the Book of Revelation, Babylon is personified and then described as evil, and God will destroy it.

Babylon could be an actual physical place, perhaps a person, or something different. Some Bible teachers say that Babylon must physically be rebuilt, but that seems a challenging task. According to them, it will be rebuilt during seven years of tribulation, and then its destruction will come. It is not easy to see how a mighty city could be built from nothing in seven years to a point where it becomes the center of the world's politics and commerce.

Another position is that Babylon is one of the leading cities in the world, like Rome, London, or Washington D.C. Who knows?

A third interpretation is that Babylon is symbolic, meaning the spirit of Babylon controls the world's political and economic systems. In ancient Babylon, its religious system was polytheistic, that is, many gods. In Babylon, there were temples to different gods everywhere, and people could pick and choose the gods they worshiped. In other words, they packaged their own belief systems. That turned each person into a little god. Today, that's the world we live in, where everyone constructs their truth, and truth is relative. It is a rejection of the idea that there is an ultimate unwavering Truth. This relativistic belief system is the antithesis of the belief in an unchanging 'God Almighty.' The Book of Revelation says that Babylon will fall, as well as the commercial system created from it, and people will weep and curse God.

Is there anything else you might share about The Last Jerusalem?

Obviously, it is fictional. Read the Bible to get the entire actual story.

Reading Group Guide

1. Character Connections: Which character's journey or transformation resonated with you the most, and why?

2. Faith: How does the theme of faith manifest throughout the story, especially in the face of adversity and uncertainty? How is Thomas's faith strengthened during this story, and where does he put his faith?

3. Symbolism: What do you think the recurring motif of the desert signifies in the story, both metaphorically and literally?

4. Spiritual Themes: In what ways does the story explore spiritual beliefs, prophecy, and divine intervention? How do these elements impact the characters' actions and decisions?

5. End Times: The theme of the end times reoccurs throughout this story. Are we in the end times, and why? What is your response to this?

6. Cultural Exploration: How does the story delve into the Jewish, Bedouin, and Aramean Christian cultures, traditions, and ways of life? What aspects were particularly intriguing or enlightening for you?

7. The Impact of War: Reflect on how the story portrays the effects of war on individuals and communities, especially what will happen to this world with the last battle, known as the Battle of Armageddon.

8. Fate, Divine Providence, and Free Will: How does free will intersect in the characters' decisions and the unfolding events? Can you identify pivotal moments where their choices altered the course of the story?

About the Author

I grew up in the United States but now live in Europe, splitting my time between a house overlooking the sea in Spain and a chalet in the Swiss Alps. I have written numerous novels, novellas, and short stories in different genres. You can find out more at www.casstell.com.

Other Books by Cass Tell

Naked Island: Would you survive a show like Naked and Afraid? What if the real dangers happened when the cameras were turned off?

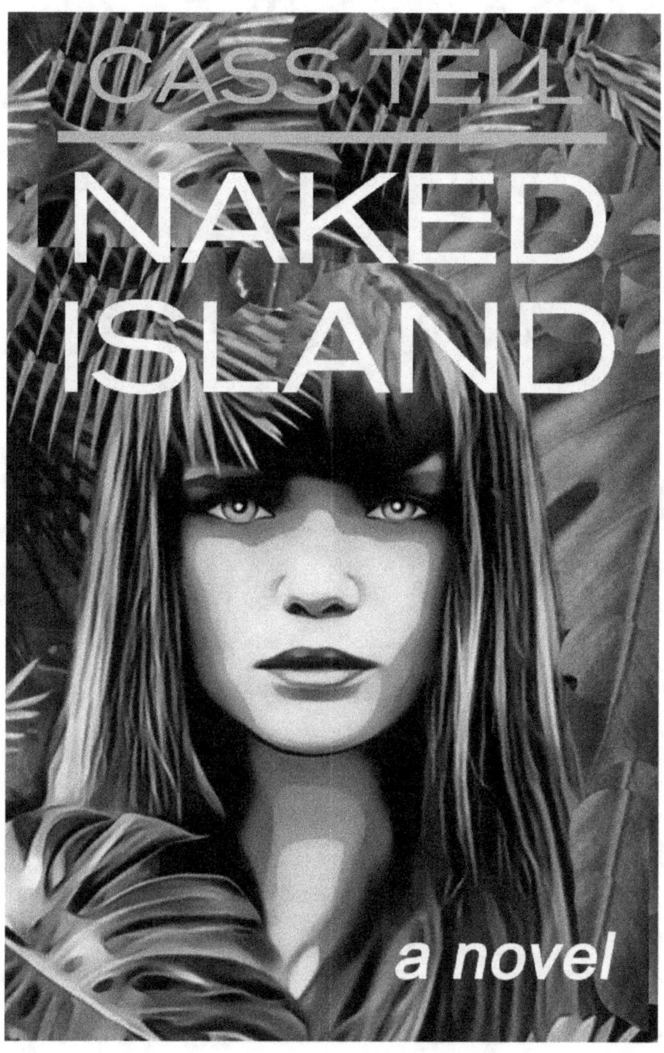

The Savant - a novel. What if you could predict future events? Enjoy The SAVANT, a profound and compelling story that follows the journey of a gifted child with a unique form of 'savant syndrome.'

Faraway Lands: A gripping historical novel of adventure where worlds collide during the treacherous French Revolution. Can two souls survive as the French Revolution brutally eliminates anyone with opposing views?

9 781938 367915